Estate In Peril

The Mystery Book Nook - Book 2

Sue Hollowell

Estate in Peril

Copyright © 2023 by Sue Hollowell

All rights reserved.

No portion of this book may be reproduced in any form without written permission from the publisher or author, except as permitted by U.S. copyright law.

Contents

CHAPTER ONE	1
CHAPTER TWO	11
CHAPTER THREE	22
CHAPTER FOUR	33
CHAPTER FIVE	43
CHAPTER SIX	54
CHAPTER SEVEN	64
CHAPTER EIGHT	74
CHAPTER NINE	84
CHAPTER TEN	94
CHAPTER ELEVEN	105
CHAPTER TWELVE	116
CHAPTER THIRTEEN	126
CHAPTER FOURTEEN	136
CHAPTER FIFTEEN	149
About the Author	156

CHAPTER ONE

"Turn left at the light." I pointed in the direction we needed to get to The Pecan Patch, the café advertising "'world famous pecan pie.'" My stomach grumbled right on cue. Our last stop had been hours ago, and my hunger let me know it.

Maude swiftly made the turn, as I gestured toward the sign of the café. Relief in sight, both for my stomach and my tired rear end. When Maude suggested this road trip from Cedarbrook to visit her son and daughter-in-law, I had visions of Thelma and Louise. The reality was less so, but every day with Maude was an adventure. Gently pulling to a stop, Maude turned off the engine as it clicked to cool off in the heat of the day.

Port la Pena sat in the Golden Triangle of Southeast Texas. I saw the distant ocean twinkling in the sun. A much different vision than my home on the Oregon coast.

I peeled myself off the seat and stepped into the warmth, stretching my achy old bones. I patted the car we affectionately called The Detective Mobile. The nearby shops looked like they could have been from the 1950s. "This is cute," I said.

"The café is new since I left town. But Nathan said it's great," Maude said. After settling in, we planned to visit Nathan and his wife, Mollie, the next day.

The cool air of the café shocked my warm face. I took a moment to appreciate the charming atmosphere. The warm aroma of freshly brewed coffee mingled with the sweet scent of that promised famous pie.

"Hello, ladies. Two?" the hostess asked.

We both nodded and followed her to a booth. "Can I get you some sweet tea?" she said as she placed the menus in front of us.

"Oh, yes!" Maude said. "You have to try it, Mabel."

I would take any cold beverage I could get right about now. I grabbed the menu and fanned my face.

"Let's order pie first," Maude suggested. The adventure with her just got better every time. "Then if we want to have a salad, we can."

Hearing my mother's voice in my head saying you can't have dessert unless you eat your vegetables, I shook my head. Some habits die hard.

"Well, I'm going to," she replied. Following suit, we both ordered a large slice of pie. Because, I mean, why not?

That woman had become a significant influence in my life since we met on our Carson family vacation in Hollywerth. I still had to pinch myself that she had moved to Cedarbrook and we had opened our own investigative agency. While other women our age enjoyed quiet retirement, we craved adventure. There was nothing quite like the rush of danger and the satisfaction of bringing a culprit to justice. And Maude's background and connections in cybersecurity didn't hurt.

"Ah, this is nice," I mused aloud, taking in the cozy ambiance before my gaze returned to Maude.

She leaned forward, her chin resting on her hand as she studied the café patrons with a hawk-like intensity. Was she ever not in detective mode? I think her days of internet sleuthing ruined her for just enjoying the moment.

"OK, Maude. What is it?" I knew by now she was several steps ahead of me.

"First of all," she began, tapping her finger on the table, "the barista over there has been sneaking bites of the blueberry scones when she thinks nobody's watching." She gave a slight nod of her head toward the corner counter.

"Scandalous!" I said, feigning shock.

Maude chuckled and sat back in her seat as the waitress brought the biggest pieces of pie I had ever seen, dripping with vanilla ice cream. There wouldn't be room for even the smallest vegetable after I devoured this treat. "OK. I'll dial it back," she said. "Our major goal with this trip was family time with Nathan and Mollie."

"I can't wait to meet them," I said, diving into the pie. I had made plenty of pies in my years, but nothing compared to this.

"They're excited to meet you, too."

Pointing to the pie, I said, "What makes this so much better than every other pecan pie I've ever had?" I poked it apart to examine the ingredients, suspecting I tasted dark chocolate.

"Bourbon," Maude confidently said.

Now that she mentioned it, I tasted a hint of the alcohol that cooked up as caramel and toffee flavors. We would have to stop back here on our way out of town for a pie to go. Maybe I could sweet talk the recipe out of the cook.

As we finished our tea and pie, I couldn't help but notice a quaint little shop across the street. The sign hanging above the door read "The Mystery Book Nook" in charming, cursive lettering. I nudged Maude's arm and gestured towards it. "Look at that, Maude," I said, my voice barely louder than a whisper. "A mystery bookstore right across the street. What are the odds?"

"Coincidence or fate?" Maude mused, her eyes narrowing as she observed the store. "Either way, I think we should pay them a visit."

"Agreed," I replied, suddenly feeling a thrill of excitement course through me.

We paid our bill, thanked the waitress with a promise to return, and made our way across the street. As we stepped onto the sidewalk, I couldn't shake the feeling that this was more than just a simple coincidence. It was as if the universe was conspiring to lead us to the perfect location for our detective work.

"Maude, do you ever feel like the world is just too perfectly aligned sometimes?" I asked, glancing over at her as we crossed the road.

"More often than not," she replied with a wink. "But I've learned not to question these things. Instead, I embrace them and see where they take me." Her philosophy had proved true from the first day we had met.

"Spoken like a true detective," I teased, and we both shared a laugh before pushing open the door to the bookstore.

The bell above the door jingled cheerfully, announcing our arrival. We were greeted by the smell of cinnamon spice. Rows upon rows of bookshelves stretched out before us, each one filled with mystery novels that seemed to beckon us from their spots on the shelves.

"Wow," I breathed, my eyes scanning the titles as we wandered through the store. "This place is like a treasure trove for people like us."

"Indeed," Maude agreed, running her fingers along the spines of several books as we walked. "I can't help but wonder what secrets these pages hold."

"Only one way to find out," I said, pulling a book from the shelf at random and flipping it open. Moving to a nearby overstuffed chair, I plopped down and read through several pages. With the extensive number of mystery books in this place, you might never get us out of here. This could be good training for our detective business. I closed the book and placed it on my lap, gazing at the full floor-to-ceiling shelves. What a great day. Pecan pie to die for, and a bookstore dedicated to amateur sleuths.

Maude approached me and said, "We might just have to move here. Excuse me," she called out, seeking the attention of the two women behind the counter. The older woman looked up from her book with a welcoming smile. Beside her stood a young woman, her long dark hair in a ponytail bouncing as she eagerly awaited our inquiry.

"Welcome to The Mystery Book Nook," said the older woman, extending her hand. She looked super comfortable wearing some leggings with a shirt over them. "I'm Vangie Guillory, the owner."

"Nice to meet you, Vangie," I replied, shaking her hand warmly. "I'm Mabel, and this is my friend, Maude."

Maude gazed around. "This is impressive. I've never seen a bookstore dedicated to only mystery books. Right up our alley." She pointed at me.

"Ah, fellow mystery enthusiasts," Vangie said, her eyes sparkling with curiosity. "I hope you enjoy our humble store."

"Speaking of which," Maude interjected, "is there a local section? Somewhere we might find books about Port la Pena's history, legends, or unsolved mysteries?"

"Of course," replied the younger woman, stepping forward. "I'm Erin McCarthy, by the way. Follow me, and I'll show you the way." Erin's cowgirl boots clunked along the floor.

Maude and I giggled like schoolgirls.

Erin guided us through the labyrinth of shelves. "Here we are," she announced, stopping before a small section labeled "'Local Lore.'" She gestured grandly at the tightly packed shelves. "You'll find everything you need right here."

"Excellent," Maude muttered, already scanning the titles.

"Let me know if there's something specific you're looking for," Erin said and left us to our own devices.

"Let's see," I mused, pulling a book from the shelf and flipping through its pages. "Port la Pena: History, Hauntings, and Homicides." My eyebrows shot up in excitement. "Do you remember any of these stories from when you lived here?"

"Not much," she said. "I was traveling a lot for work back in the day." She snatched a book of her own. "The Curious Case of the Smuggler's Cove."

"Sounds thrilling." I grinned, adding it to our growing pile.

The bell jingled on the front door as more customers entered the bookstore. A couple approached Erin as she pointed them to a back room.

"Remember, Maude," I said. Her gaze was serious as she looked me in the eye. "We're not here for business. We're here to enjoy time with your son and his wife."

She nodded solemnly, though a playful smirk tugged at the corner of her mouth. "Of course. But there's no harm in enjoying ourselves along the way, is there?"

I rolled my eyes, but couldn't suppress a smile. "No, I suppose not," I relented, pulling another book from the shelf. My mind wandered as we immersed ourselves in the lore of Port la Pena.

Vangie approached us, her eyes bright with anticipation. "I couldn't help but notice your enthusiasm for mysteries," she said, a secretive smile playing on her lips. "Would you be interested in learning about our mystery-solving club?"

"Club?" Maude echoed, curiosity piqued.

"Indeed," Vangie continued, leaning in conspiratorially. "We're a group of like-minded individuals who gather to discuss and solve local mysteries. We meet twice a month to share our findings, exchange theories, and piece together the puzzles that Port la Pena offers."

"Does this mean we get to wear detective hats and trench coats?" I asked in mock seriousness, earning a chuckle from Vangie.

"Only if you want to," she replied. "The club is open to anyone with a passion for detective work and a mind sharp enough to cut through the fog of deception."

"Sounds like fun!" I declared, clapping my hands together. "What do you think, Maude? Shall we give it a go?"

The nature of the club might be too amateur for Maude and her expertise in cybersecurity. But it might be a fun hobby to try that could help us hone our skills.

She nodded. I could see the wheels already in high gear.

"Excellent!" Vangie exclaimed, clearly pleased to have found kindred spirits. "Erin can get you all set up."

"Thank you, Vangie," I replied, beaming. "We're looking forward to it!"

Maude and I exchanged glances, excitement bubbling between us like champagne. Who knew what secrets the mystery-solving club might hold? One thing was certain: our adventure in Port la Pena had just taken a decidedly thrilling turn.

"Detective hats and trench coats," Maude mused, shaking her head as we made our purchases. "You really are incorrigible, Mabel."

"Guilty as charged," I admitted cheerfully, my heart swelling with anticipation. The game, as they say, was afoot!

CHAPTER TWO

I smiled at Vangie as she reappeared from behind a towering stack of colorful, leather-bound books. "Tell me more about the members of this mystery-solving club."

Maude, who had been examining an old, slender volume on codes and ciphers, turned her keen gaze towards us.

"Of course!" Vangie enthused. "Our group has grown lately, and we're made up of a diverse range of individuals. Each member brings their own unique skills and perspective to the table."

"Any fellow octogenarians?" Maude inquired, one silver eyebrow arched.

"Actually, yes! Our oldest member is a retired detective named Stan," Vangie replied, grinning. "He's sharp as a tack and full of fascinating stories about his time on the force."

"Sounds like a character," I mused, imagining the lively conversations that must take place at these gatherings. "What about the rest of the club?"

"Well, there's Erin, of course," Vangie said, nodding towards the young woman who was currently helping another customer at the front counter. "She is learning forensic psychology - she's got a real knack for getting inside the minds of criminals."

"Ooh, intriguing," I murmured, my interest piqued. As if sensing our attention, Erin glanced over and gave us a friendly wave.

"Then there's Jack," Vangie continued. "He's a bit of a tech whiz - always tinkering with gadgets and coming up with inventive ways to gather information. And last but not least, we have London, our resident historian. She's adept at uncovering long-buried secrets."

Maude frowned thoughtfully, her fingers drumming against the spine of the book she still held. "I can see how such a diverse group might prove helpful in solving mysteries," she conceded.

"Exactly!" Vangie agreed, clapping her hands together. "We complement each other's abilities and work together as a team. It's quite remarkable, really."

Maude's eyes widened with fascination. I could tell she was becoming more and more intrigued by the idea of joining this eclectic group of amateur sleuths. "It just might be worth our while to attend one of these meetings," she mused aloud, her voice soft, as if testing the waters.

"Indeed," I chimed in, my excitement coursing through me like electricity. The thought of being among fellow detectives, all searching for clues to solve mysteries, sent a thrill down my spine. "If nothing else, it will give us a chance to make some valuable connections and gather intel that could aid us in our future investigations."

"Very well," Maude said, closing the book on cryptography with a decisive snap that echoed throughout the room. "We shall attend this meeting and see what we can learn."

"Fantastic!" Vangie cried, delighted by our decision. She leaned forward conspiratorially, her dark eyes glinting with curiosity. "I'm certain you'll find it most enlightening." Her smile was as broad as her enthusiasm.

As we were checking out, my mind buzzed with anticipation. Port la Pena was full of mystery; anything could happen here. –Our adventure in Port la Pena had just become infinitely more interesting.

"Before we go," I said, turning back to Vangie and Erin, "for the club that focuses on local stories. Is there a book you would recommend us reading?"

Vangie and Erin exchanged a quick glance. "Well, we have people from all over the world on the forum," Erin replied carefully. "But our group enjoys focusing on the local stories." She led us to a section filled with dusty tomes, their spines cracked and faded with age.

"Ah," she said, pulling out a thick volume titled *'Port la Pena: A History of Intrigue.'* "This book details some of the most baffling cases and unsolved mysteries of our town's past." She passed it to me, her voice tinged with enthusiasm. "I think it should give you plenty of background information."

Maude took the book from Erin appreciatively, running her hand across the soft leather cover. Her eyes scanned the table of contents, her curiosity piqued.

As Maude continued her perusal, an odd little book caught my eye. The cover was adorned with peculiar symbols and cryptic text. "What's this?" I asked, picking it up with interest.

"Oh, that's a fascinating find," Vangie said, leaning in to get a better look. "It's an old cipher book, used by spies and secret societies throughout history. Some believe it has connections to Port la Pena's shadowy past."

"Interesting," I mused, feeling a shiver of excitement run down my spine. "Perhaps it will come in handy as we delve deeper into the secrets of this town."

"Indeed it might," Maude agreed, her eyes alight with enthusiasm. "We shall add it to our collection of resources."

With our new acquisitions in hand, we made our way to the front of the store. As Erin rang up our purchases, Maude struck up a conversation with Vangie.

"Tell me, Vangie, have you ever encountered any unusual or unexplainable events in Port la Pena?" Maude asked, her keen eyes studying the bookstore owner.

"Ah, well," Vangie began, a wistful smile playing on her lips. "I suppose my life has been filled with more than its fair share of enigmas and peculiar happenings. But that's what makes it all so thrilling, wouldn't you agree?"

"Indeed," Maude concurred. "A life devoid of mystery would be dreadfully dull."

After paying for our books, we bid farewell to Vangie and Erin, promising to return soon for the mystery-solving club meeting. As we stepped out into the warm afternoon air, I couldn't help but feel a renewed sense of purpose.

"Maude," I said as we strolled down the sidewalk, "I believe we've stumbled upon something truly extraordinary here in Port la Pena. And I can't wait to see where this adventure takes us next."

We silently drove to our cottage. Maude had booked us a small place right on the beach. I stepped out of the car, thinking I might actually see myself living here. I would miss my daughters and son greatly in Cedarbrook, especially now that we were just beginning to reconnect. The warmth of the sun massaged my aching muscles. Living in a more tropical place was quite attractive, leaving the harsh winters in Cedarbrook.

Heaving our luggage from the trunk, we headed to the door. Maude punched the code in, and the door swung open. The entire place was covered in beach decor. I loved it, feeling relaxation wash over me. Moving my bag to the side, I proceeded to the sliding glass doors that opened to a small deck facing the beach.

"I think we need a trip to the store for the fixings for umbrella drinks," Maude said.

Plopping into a chair, I shaded my eyes toward the water. "This is beautiful," I said. "Why did you leave?"

Maude joined me on the deck. We hadn't much talked about her former life. We'd been focused on the here and now.

Quietly, she started. "When Charlie passed, I couldn't bear the memories."

Oh, my heart clenched. I had no idea.

"I guess you could say I've been avoiding it since then, afraid the pain would be too much."

I put my hand on her arm. "Maude, I'm so sorry."

She shrugged. "I've been back to visit Nathan. But…"

Now I felt silly, suggesting all of these local excursions when my friend was struggling with her memories.

"If it's too much, we can make it a quick visit with Nathan and go. We don't have to go to the mystery club."

She smiled at me, a twinkle in her eye. "Mysteries are my passion. We are definitely going to the club. And that might just be what can help me heal."

We hadn't stopped at the store for any groceries. "Would you like to head out for a meal?"

Maude nodded wistfully.

While the tea and pie were fun to splurge on, my body was craving some protein and vegetables. "I saw a place called The Saucy Piglet that looked like they had barbecue," I suggested.

Without a word, she went inside and got her purse.

"Why don't you let me drive this time?" I offered.

The tone of excitement had significantly dampened. I was at a loss for how to help my friend.

Maude silently got into the passenger seat. "I'll be OK. Frankly, I think all of this is therapeutic."

Several blocks later, we had arrived. Country music blared from a jukebox in the corner. The waitress dressed in adorable cowgirl attire, led us to our table and shared the specials of the day. The diner was decorated with cowgirl memorabilia, leather chaps, and memorabilia of the old west. One wall carried an old saddle and saddle bags. The wooden tables were covered in red and white checked tablecloths. The ceiling gave the impression of a wooden barn.

An old man sat at a nearby table and tipped his cowboy hat toward us. Sauce stained a napkin tucked into the collar of his shirt. He raised his beer glass. The smell of sweet, smoky barbecue filled the air.

The waitress arrived with two beers and took our orders.

Maude held up her mug and said, "Cheers to more adventure, my friend." We clinked glasses as we watched the crowd grow for mealtime.

"I think we're in for that with the mystery club," I said.

She perked up. "How cool is that? Maybe we start one of those back home in Cedarbrook."

She had read my mind. "That would be amazing. I would love to get some of my elderly friends more active. Do something to keep their brains sharp."

"Excuse me, ma'am." The elderly man held out his hand to Maude. "May I ask you to dance?"

Maude smiled. The man still had the napkin tucked into his shirt. He looked down and quickly wrapped it up and stuffed it into his pocket. She looked at me.

"Why don't you go until our food arrives. I'll be fine," I said.

Maude took his hand as he led her to the small dance floor along the side of the room. He beamed at Maude as they danced between two empty tables, twirling her around just as the song ended. She curtsied and he bowed, kissing her hand.

She returned to our table, her face flushed. "I needed that."

The waitress arrived with our steaming plates of barbecued pork sandwiches and bowls piled high with cole slaw.

We devoured the food, my belly pooching out from the large portions. "I'm excited about the mystery club."

"Me too," Maude said, the spark returning to her eyes. I can't wait to dive into that book Vangie recommended."

"I bet you're not going to get any sleep tonight," I said.

Maude stared off into the distance. "What's on your mind?" I asked, wiping barbecue sauce from the corner of my mouth.

"That man reminds me of my late husband," she said, her voice heavy with emotion.

I reached out and placed my hand on hers. "Tell me about him."

Maude's eyes softened, and she began recounting tales of her husband's cowboy hats and love for barbecue. As she spoke, I could see the memories bringing her comfort.

"Excuse me, ladies. I couldn't help but overhear your conversation about the mystery club. I'm Stan," said the man in the cowboy hat

"Oh my gosh," Maude said. "Will you be there at the next meeting?"

"Wouldn't miss it ma'am. I've been working on a local mystery for quite some time." He dipped into his plaid shirt pocket and retrieved a piece of paper, holding it out to us.

Curious, I took the paper from him and unfolded it. It was a map, with an X marking a spot deep in the woods outside of town.

"What's this?" I asked.

"That, my dears, is the location of an old, abandoned mansion. It's said to be haunted, but there's also rumors that there's a treasure hidden within its walls. I've been searching for it myself but haven't had any luck so far," he explained.

Maude's eyes widened with excitement. I could see her holding herself back, but eager to jump right in to another adventure.

"Well, Stan, we'll see you at the club . It was nice to meet you," I said.

He bowed and tipped his hat.

Maude watched him walk away and leaned in. "That was quite something. Wasn't it?"

CHAPTER THREE

We turned onto a street lined with houses, stopping in front of a white picket fence. A porch swing swayed gently in the breeze and flowers spilled from every bed.

The front door burst open. Nathan strode out, arms open wide. "Mom! You're here!"

Tears flowed from Maude's eyes as she embraced her son. "It's wonderful to see you."

Mollie followed, enveloping her in a hug. "We've been expecting you."

"It's a pleasure to finally meet you," I said. "I'm Mabel, Maude's partner in crime."

Mollie's smile deepened. "I've heard so much about you. I'm Mollie."

We settled into Nathan and Mollie's cozy living room, sunlight filtering through lace curtains as a pot of tea steeped on the table.

Nathan leaned forward, hands clasped between his knees. "So good to see you."

"It's been too long since I saw you. A little road trip seemed in order," Maude said.

He stared at Maude as if he sensed something was up. "What else is going on?"

Maude stood and helped herself to tea, offering me some.

"Just a lot of memories here," she whispered.

Nathan approached her from behind, placing a hand on her shoulder. "I get that."

Maude returned to her chair, placing our tea in front of us.

"There's more, isn't there?" Nathan peered at his mom.

"I can't get away with anything, can I?" Maude chuckled.

"Another case?" Mollie asked.

"Not yet. We discovered that lovely Mystery Book Nook yesterday," Maude said.

Nathan sat back in his chair, laughing. "That's right up your alley, Mom."

"We do miss the excitement of your cases though," Mollie said with a teasing smile. "Nathan worries, but I find your adventures fascinating."

"Now, now." Nathan gave her a reproachful look. "Let's not encourage them."

Maude's eyes sparkled with mirth. "Oh, don't worry. We're retired. Aren't we, Mabel?"

"Of course we are," I said brightly. "Adventures are for the young."

Nathan visibly relaxed, shoulders loosening from their tense set. "Well, that's a relief." He grasped Maude's hands, eyes softening with affection. "I'm just glad to have you here, safe and sound."

"As am I." Maude squeezed his hands. She let go and reached for her tea. "The house next door is for sale?"

"Thank God," Nathan said, firmly.

Maude and I looked at each other, wondering what his tone was about. As any talented investigator does, she waited in uncomfortable silence for Nathan to continue. He fidgeted in his seat. Maude looked at Mollie, who shrugged.

"OK. That guy has been a jerk from the day he moved in," Nathan said.

Maude stepped toward the window and peeked through the curtains toward the neighbor's house. "He sure doesn't maintain his yard as nice as you do." It was obvious Mollie and Nathan spent a lot of time gardening. Their yard looked like they could feature it in a magazine.

"That's not all." Nathan stood and joined his mom. "He plays music very loud. And he has the nerve to throw garbage over the fence and claim it's not his."

Maude turned toward Nathan. "Wow. Have you called the police?"

Mollie joined them and said, "We even have a restraining order. But it's pretty tough, given he's right next door. Our only hope is that the house sells quickly, and he leaves for good."

Glancing around Nathan at me, Maude slowly said, "I think I want to look at the house."

"What?!" Nathan said. "Would you actually move back here?"

Maude resumed her seat, grabbing her tea. She shrugged. This was a new development. Maude and I had our detective agency back in Cedarbrook. Would she actually leave me to return to her home and be closer to her son? I couldn't blame her. But my heart clenched. She and I were just getting started. And frankly, I couldn't imagine my life without her. From the little I had seen about Port la Pena, I did like the town. But seriously considering a move was next level.

"It couldn't hurt to look," Maude said.

Mollie grabbed her phone and dialed. "No time like the present." She stepped to the side for her conversation with the real estate agent.

Nathan chuckled. "You always keep me on my toes, Mom."

I could only imagine how it must have been growing up with her.

"Gina was in the neighborhood. She'll be here in just a few to let you in," Mollie said. She looked at Nathan. "You'll have to go by yourselves, of course. Though I don't know if Kenneth is home right now."

"We'll be sure to report back," Maude said. She clapped her hands as her eyes twinkled. I had no idea where this would go. But I hoped it worked out the way my friend wanted it to.

We all turned our heads as a car arrived in the driveway. Mollie peeked out and confirmed, "Gina's here."

Maude grabbed my hand as we exited the house, Mollie and Nathan behind us.

Gina raised her hand as she greeted us. "Hi, all. Glad you called."

Nathan introduced us as Gina smiled and said, "Not sure if Kenneth is home. But let's go see."

We followed Gina to the road and up Kenneth's driveway. I glanced around. Tall dandelions swayed in the breeze, their bright yellow petals spread open wide. Nearby, a patch of daisies struggled to survive in between tall spikes of crabgrass. Everywhere I looked, there were clusters of weeds determined to take over his yard.

Gina spotted me studying the mess. "Don't worry about that. He'll be cleaning that up before he moves." She knocked on the door.

Maude and I stood behind her, waiting, not hearing a sound from inside the house. Probably just as well if the owner wasn't home to entertain the mother of the person who had a restraining order against him.

Gina opened the lockbox and pulled out the key. "Be prepared for a bit of a mess inside, too." She turned the key and slowly opened the door. "Kenneth?"

Probably good to confirm he wasn't here. We certainly didn't want to surprise anyone.

As we stepped into the house, a musty odor hit my nose. The living room was dimly lit, the curtains drawn shut. We followed Gina as she led the way, her footsteps echoing through the empty house. A layer of dust coated the furniture, and the floorboards creaked beneath our feet. I couldn't help but feel a sense of unease wash over me, as if we were intruding on someone's private space.

Maude walked ahead, her eyes scanning the room. "It needs work," she said, her voice barely above a whisper.

I nodded. "It's definitely a fixer-upper."

We continued through the house, passing through the kitchen and down the hallway. The bedrooms were small, with peeling wallpaper and stained carpets. I couldn't imagine anyone living in such conditions.

As we made our way to the back of the house, we heard a faint rustling noise.

Gina froze in her tracks. "Did you hear that?"

Maude and I exchanged a worried look as we followed Gina to the source of the noise. We stepped into a small room at the back of the house. A small mouse scurried from the room. The sight before us made my heart skip a beat.

There, lying on the floor, was Kenneth. His face was twisted in pain, his body covered in bruises. Maude rushed over to him, checking for a pulse. I could see the fear in her eyes as she turned to us.

"He's dead," she said, her voice trembling.

Gina pulled out her phone and dialed 911 as we all stood there, stunned and horrified. The musty smell of the house was now mixed with the metallic scent of blood, and I felt bile rise in my throat.

Who could have done this? Was it someone from the neighborhood? Or was it a stranger who had broken in? The questions swirled in my head, but one thing was clear — we had stumbled upon a murder scene.

As we waited for the police to arrive, I couldn't help but think that our time in Port la Pena had just taken a dire turn. There was no way we couldn't get involved in this.

I glanced at Maude as she turned to look at me. She tilted her head toward the door. We left the room as Gina continued the call with the 911 operator.

"Maude, are you thinking what I'm thinking?"

She sighed, clearly on the same page as I was. With Nathan's restraining order against Kenneth, he would be a prime suspect. This wasn't good.

"No way," Maude said.

I nodded. "We have to do something. We can't just sit back and wait for the police to arrest Nathan."

Maude's eyes flickered with determination. "We need to find out who did this. We need to clear Nathan's name."

I felt a sense of relief wash over me at her words. We couldn't just let Nathan be accused of a crime he didn't commit. But the question remained — who had killed Kenneth?

"You're right. We can't just let this go. But we have to be careful. We don't want to make things worse," I said.

The musty air of the house prompted my nose to itch. "Why don't we go outside and get some fresh air while we wait for the police to arrive?" I said.

Maude slowly opened the door as it squealed in protest. So much for a fantasy of buying the house next door to Nathan.

The warm air blasted us as we picked our way through overgrown weeds infringing upon the sidewalk. We reached the road and turned toward the house.

I glanced at Nathan's house and saw Mollie wave to us through the large front window. Oh boy. Things were about to drastically change their lives. Grabbing Maude's hand, I squeezed.

Gina appeared on the doorstep, wiping her nose and dabbing her eyes with a tissue. This must be an agent's worst nightmare. And they probably had to deal with some nasty things. Not a job I would want. Running the Treehouse Hotel brought some interesting situations, but we had yet to deal with a murder in one of our units.

She held out her phone to us, saying, "The police are on their way." Turning to face the house, she continued her sniffles.

I gently placed my hand on her back. "I'm so sorry."

Shaking her head, she said, "It's not your fault. And frankly, I'm not surprised."

That was quite the callous comment. Nobody deserved to be murdered. What did Gina know about Kenneth?

She continued, "He's really upset a lot of people lately and owed them a lot of money. That's why he was selling his house."

Quickly looking back at Maude and I, she clamped her mouth shut, realizing she probably had said too much.

We remained silent, the oldest detective trick in the book.

As if right on cue, Gina backtracked her statements. "I shouldn't speak ill of the dead. He was trying, but he was completely underwater with his finances."

The sound of sirens grew louder. We knew the police would soon be on the scene, and we had to act fast.

"Let's head back to Mollie's house," Maude said. "Gina, we'll be right next door."

She withdrew another tissue from her bag, sniffling and nodding. "OK."

As we walked back, my mind raced with possibilities. Who could have killed Kenneth, and why? And how could we prove Nathan's innocence?

Mollie spotted us on our return and met us at the door.

"How was it," she asked, bouncing from excitement. "Pretty nasty, I bet, from judging the state of the yard."

That was saying it mildly.

"Can we get you two a refill of your tea?" Nathan asked as we entered the living room. "Wait. What's wrong, Mom?"

Maude took his hand and sat him down on the couch. "Nathan, we need to talk. Kenneth has been murdered."

CHAPTER FOUR

Nathan looked between Maude and I, his brows furrowed. "What?"

"I'm sorry," Maude said, rubbing Nathan's hands.

He bolted up, pacing the room. "How?"

Shock covered his face. Mollie joined him and guided him back to his seat.

"Gina found his body. It wasn't pretty," Maude said.

Nathan ran his hand through his hair. "I can't believe it."

"Hon, take a deep breath," Mollie said. "He's been a burr in the side of our quiet community for years. His loud arguments with neighbors and questionable business dealings…" She shook her head.

A light knock came from the front door, startling us all.

Maude squeezed her eyes tight, bracing for what would likely be police questioning.

Nathan took a deep breath and stood up, his eyes still wide with shock. He walked over to the door and opened it, revealing two police officers standing on the other side.

"Mr. Henly, we need to ask you a few questions," one officer said, his voice stern.

Nathan nodded and stepped aside, allowing the officers to enter. They walked into the living room and took a seat on the couch, while Nathan and Maude sat across from them.

"We understand you had a restraining order against Kenneth," one of them stated, looking up from his notepad.

Nathan nodded again, his eyes downcast. "Yes, I did. It was a few years ago, after he threatened my family."

The officers jotted down notes, their expressions unreadable. Mollie sat next to Nathan, rubbing his back in a soothing motion.

"Did you see or hear anything suspicious last night?" the first officer asked, looking up from his notes.

Nathan shook his head. "No, we didn't hear anything. We were asleep."

The second officer leaned forward. "Are you sure? Any little detail, no matter how insignificant, could help us with our investigation."

Nathan thought for a moment, his brow furrowed in concentration. "Actually, now that you mention it, I did see a car parked outside around midnight. It was a dark sedan, I think."

The officers scribbled down more notes, nodding their heads in acknowledgment.

"Thank you for your cooperation," the first officer said, standing up. "We'll be in touch if we need anything else."

After their questioning, the detectives left, leaving Nathan and his family in stunned silence. Maude and Mollie exchanged worried glances, both unsure of what to say.

Nathan finally spoke up, his voice shaking. "I can't believe he's really gone. Even with everything he did to me, I never wished him dead."

Mollie put her arm around Nathan's shoulders, pulling him close. "I know, hon. No one deserves to die like that."

Maude caught my attention with a slight nod. Knowing exactly what she meant, I was completely on board. Our initial purpose for a fun adventure to Port la Pena had quickly turned into a serious murder investigation. One in which Maude's family was integrally involved.

This would be our most important case yet.

"Maude," I stood and gestured for her to follow me into the kitchen.

I put my hands on her shoulders and walked her into the kitchen, where I could speak to her out of earshot of Nathan and Mollie. "Maude, it could be dangerous up against a murderer. We have to be careful."

She glanced over her shoulder at Nathan and Mollie as she followed me.

"Mabel, I'm at a loss."

"Take a deep breath. This is our specialty. We have to put our logical hats on and approach this just as we have all of our other cases." I reached a hand out to her. "We'll figure it out."

"I wish I had your confidence." Maude sighed heavily and fell into one of the chairs around the table. "This gives me a whole new perspective of the other side of an investigation," Maude said.

Nathan and Mollie joined us in the kitchen. "Mom, you are not on duty for this case. You need to leave it to the professionals," Nathan said.

I knew that was the last thing she intended to do. And Nathan probably knew that, too.

Maude kept silent. You could hear a pin drop. "I have a few thoughts," she whispered, waiting for Nathan's response.

"I know you can't help yourself. But please share those with the police and let them do their job," Nathan pleaded.

Maude nodded, but I could tell she wasn't convinced. I touched her hand lightly, giving her a reassuring smile.

"Don't worry. We'll help in any way we can, but we'll also make sure to stay out of the way of the police investigation," I said.

Nathan seemed to relax slightly at my words. "Thank you, Mabel. I appreciate your help, but I don't want anyone to get hurt."

Mollie chimed in, "Yes, we don't want to put anyone in danger."

Maude nodded again, her expression thoughtful. "I understand, and I'll be careful. But I have a feeling there's more to this than meets the eye."

I could tell she was itching to dive into the investigation, but for now, we had to respect Nathan's wishes and let the police do their job.

"Why don't we give Nathan and Mollie some space?" I said. Maude and I couldn't do anything until we had a chance to put our heads together.

As we left Nathan's house, Maude was deep in thought, lost in her own world. I knew she was working out a plan in her head. We walked in silence until we reached the car.

"Maude, what are you thinking?" I asked, buckling my seatbelt.

She chuckled to herself quietly before answering me. "I need to do some digging," she said, starting the car.

"What kind of digging?" I asked, my curiosity piqued.

"I want to know more about Kenneth's business dealings. If he was involved in anything shady, it could have led to his murder," she said, her eyes focused on the road ahead.

"That's a good point. Where do you want to start?" I asked.

"What do you think about driving around a bit so we can see some sights and I can clear my head?" she said, flooring the gas pedal and causing us both to lurch forward against our seat belts.

I couldn't help but laugh at Maude's sudden change of topic. "Sure, I'm always up for a little sightseeing," I replied, adjusting my seatbelt so I could breathe again.

We drove through the streets of Port la Pena, taking in the sights and sounds of the town. Maude drove with a purpose, her eyes scanning the buildings and streets for anything that might catch her attention.

As we drove down a particularly rundown street, we saw a group of people gathered on the sidewalk. A man was ranting and raving about something, waving his arms wildly.

"Let's stop and see what's going on," Maude said, pulling over to the side of the road.

We got out of the car and made our way over to the crowd. As we got closer, we could hear the man's words more clearly.

"They're trying to shut us down! They're trying to take away our livelihoods!"

Maude turned to me, a glint in her eye, never one to let her curiosity sit idle.

We approached the man, who immediately stopped his ranting and looked at us suspiciously.

"What do you want?" he asked, crossing his arms defensively.

"We're just curious about what's going on here," I said, trying to appear friendly.

The man seemed to soften slightly. "They're trying to shut down our bar," he said, gesturing to a dingy building behind him. "They say they want more upscale businesses with the new development coming in. But we've been here for years!"

Maude hesitated before walking away, her eyes scanning the decrepit building that loomed overhead. The stone facade was stained with years of neglect and graffiti, each mark a testament to the passage of time. Cracks snaked through the walls like veins, threatening to split the entire structure apart.

As Maude examined the building, a sudden realization dawned on her. She turned to me, her eyes sparkling with excitement.

"Mabel, this could be the key to our investigation," she said, a hint of excitement in her voice.

"What do you mean?" I asked, confused.

"Well, think about it. Kenneth was a developer, right? And this bar is in the way of the new development coming in. What if someone wanted to get rid of it to make way for the new project?" Maude said, her mind racing with possibilities.

"I see what you're getting at," I replied, nodding my head. "But how can we prove it?"

Maude's eyes lit up with an idea. "We'll have to do some more digging, but I'm sure there's a paper trail somewhere. We just have to find it."

As we left the bar and made our way back to the car, Maude was already deep in thought, her mind racing with possibilities. I knew she wouldn't rest until she had found the answers she was looking for.

"Maude, how do you think this is related to Kenneth's murder?" I asked, as we got back in the car.

"If someone was willing to go to such lengths to get rid of a bar, who's to say they wouldn't do the same to a person?" she replied, her eyes focused on the road ahead.

I couldn't argue with her logic. There was more to this case than met the eye, and Maude was determined to get to the bottom of it.

We drove around for a while longer, Maude lost in thought and me pondering the possibilities of what we had just discovered. As we rounded a corner, we saw a man standing on the sidewalk with a sign that read "Save Our Homes."

Maude pulled over to the curb and rolled down her window. "Excuse me, sir, what's going on here?" she asked.

The man leaned in, his eyes bright with passion. "The developers are trying to buy up our homes and tear them down to build their fancy new condos," he said, holding up his sign for emphasis.

Maude's eyes narrowed as she listened to the man's words. "Do you know who these developers are?" she asked.

The man shook his head. "No, but they're offering us pennies on the dollar for our homes. We can't afford to live anywhere else in this town."

Maude's expression turned serious. "Thank you for telling us about this. We'll look into it," she said, rolling up the window and pulling away from the curb.

As we drove away, I could see the fire in Maude's eyes. She was determined to find out who was behind this and put a stop to their plans.

"Mabel, I need to tell you something," she said, her voice serious.

I could tell that this was important. "What is it?"

"My gut is telling me this development is related to Kenneth's murder," she said, her eyes locked on mine.

I sat there in shock, trying to process what she had just said. Did it make sense? It was also a huge accusation.

I nodded in agreement, impressed by Maude's dedication to the case. "Where do we start?" I asked.

"First, we need to gather all the information we have and go through it carefully. Then, we'll start digging online and see what we can find. I also want to talk to some people in town and see if they know anything about these developers," Maude replied.

In a short amount of time, the complexity of the case had escalated exponentially. Maude puttered around the streets as we observed more signs asking for their homes and businesses to be saved.

Reaching her arm across me, she pointed at a store called The Curiosity Cabinet, nestled in the corner, a beacon of peculiar treasures and oddities. "Let's stop in there and ask some questions. I want to make sure we have enough details for our investigation." She quickly pulled the car into a spot. The shop's windows displayed an array of antique trinkets that lured us in like moths to a flame. I pushed open the shop's creaky door, the bell overhead announcing our arrival.

CHAPTER FIVE

A tall man with a gray beard that gave him the air of an eccentric wizard greeted us. "Hello ladies. What brings you here today?"

I grinned at the man. "We're just browsing around for some knick-knacks." I didn't want to come on too strong to someone we just met.

"Speak for yourself," Maude chimed in, her eyes narrowed as she surveyed the dusty shelves. She was my best friend and business partner, sharper than a tack even in her eighties. Maude's idea of relaxation often involved solving a tricky case or decoding encrypted messages.

"Feel free to look around," the man offered, polishing a brass lamp with an intricate design. "My name is Marty. You never know what you might find in this place."

"Such as another mystery?" I mused, my curiosity piqued. As a detective duo, Maude and I had stumbled upon more than one baffling case. "I'm Mabel. This is Maude." I gestured to Maude weaving a path along the aisles.

"Or perhaps a hidden treasure," Maude added, her skepticism clear as she continued her hunt through the musty aisles. Did she think we would get more details from the items on the shelves?

"Ah, yes," Marty chuckled. "Every object has a story to tell, whether it's a dusty tome filled with arcane knowledge, or a porcelain tea set once owned by a noble family."

I marveled at a silver teapot, its polished surface reflecting the dim lighting of the shop. "It's amazing how objects can hold so much history and emotion."

"Indeed," Marty agreed. "And sometimes, they hold secrets, too."

"Secrets?" I asked, interested.

"Like that porcelain doll over there," Maude grumbled, examining the delicate figure with a critical eye. What was Maude looking for? Typically, she boldly asked questions to uncover clues. However, she seemed to browse the store like any other customer.

"Ah, you've noticed our recurring guest," Marty smirked. "She has a mysterious allure, doesn't she?"

"Or just an unsettling stare," Maude muttered, crossing her arms and raising her eyebrows at the doll.

"Perhaps both," I suggested, chuckling at their exchange. "But that's what makes this place so fascinating, right?"

"Absolutely," Marty beamed. "The Curiosity Cabinet is a haven for those seeking the unusual, the enigmatic, and the unexplained."

"Speaking of unexplained," Maude interjected, turning her attention back to Marty. "Have you heard anything about that new development project in town? It's been causing quite a stir."

"Ah, yes," Marty sighed, his shoulders slumping slightly. "I've heard rumblings about it. Seems like it could bring some unwanted changes to our quaint little community."

"Change can be good," I offered cautiously, not wanting to seem insensitive to his concerns. "Do you know who is behind the project?"

Marty reached for a salt shaker in the shape of a tree, turning it over in his hands. The ticking sound of a grandfather clock echoed through the cozy space, lending an air of timelessness to the shop. Shaking his head, he said, "It's been hard to find that out."

Maude stepped forward and said, "You don't know who it is?"

Marty stroked his chin thoughtfully, the gears in his mind clearly turning. "Well, I can't say for certain, but I've heard whispers that the developer is someone with deep pockets and influence. They might even have ties to some unsavory characters."

"Unsavory characters?" I echoed, curious. "You mean like criminals?"

"Perhaps," he said cryptically, a knowing smile playing at the corners of his mouth. "In our little town, sometimes there's often more than meets the eye."

Maude looked at me, her determination evident. "We need to find out who's behind this and what they're really after."

"True," Marty acknowledged, his eyes filled with a mix of concern and curiosity. "But be careful, ladies. You never know what dangers might lurk beneath the surface."

"Isn't that half the fun?" Maude quipped, her lips curling into a mischievous smile. "We'll be sure to keep our wits about us."

"Good," Marty replied, his voice warm and reassuring. "And if there's anything I can do, you know where to find me."

"Thanks, Marty," I said, grateful for his support. "We might just take you up on that offer."

As we exited The Curiosity Cabinet, the musty smell of old furniture faded, replaced with the fresh scent of ocean air. I glanced at Maude, her brow furrowed in concentration as she mulled over Marty's cryptic comments.

"Maude, do you think there's any merit to what Marty said? About unsavory characters and hidden agendas?" I asked, a nervous shiver running down my spine.

"Hard to say," Maude replied, her arms crossed tightly over her chest. "But if there's even a slight possibility that some sort of criminal element is involved, we need to proceed cautiously."

"Right," I agreed, swallowing hard. "We don't want to put ourselves — or anyone else — in danger."

The sudden chattering of a nearby squirrel interrupted our conversation. The animal darted across the sidewalk and propelled itself up the trunk of an oak tree. Its frantic movements seemed to mirror my own racing thoughts.

"Remember, Mabel," Maude said, her voice low and serious. "Looking into this development could lead to retaliation, sabotage, or even legal action. We need to be prepared for anything."

"Of course," I nodded, pursing my lips in determination. "We'll just have to be extra careful. After all, we've dealt with our fair share of twists and turns before."

"Indeed," Maude agreed, a brief smile flickering across her face. "Say, Mabes, what do you say we do some genuine sightseeing? Let everything we've learned so far percolate on the back burner."

We got into the car as I expected our adventures to continue. "Sounds good."

Quickly reversing out of the spot, Maude sped through the streets toward the ocean. Did I want to know where we were going?

"Just a quick pit stop first, then I'll reveal our next excursion," Maude said.

"Another fine mess you've gotten us into, Stanley," I quipped, as Maude deftly navigated the streets on our return to our cottage.

"Hardly, Ollie," Maude retorted with a smirk, her silver hair catching the sunlight blaring through the front window. "We're just getting started unraveling the tangled threads of Kenneth Andrews' murder and this whole development debacle."

I couldn't help but chuckle. Our long-standing Laurel and Hardy routine always lightened the mood, even when we were knee deep in a perplexing murder case.

"Speaking of tangled threads," I said, glancing at the growing number of protest signs scattered about town. "It seems like the residents are really knitting themselves up over this proposed development. All the more reason for us to figure out who's pulling the strings."

"Quite right," Maude agreed, her keen blue eyes scanning the signs as we passed them. "The stakes are higher than ever, and we need to stay sharp if we're going to sort out this mystery."

"Sharp, huh?" I pondered.

"You know what they say — all work and no play makes Maude a dull girl. And I don't know about you, Mabel, but I could use a little playtime myself."

After a brief stop at our quaint cottage, Maude and I arrived at Crystal Beach in high spirits. The sun was shining brightly, casting a golden glow on the soft sand as it stretched out to meet the gentle waves. Giddy children built sandcastles nearby, their laughter mingling with the cries of seagulls overhead.

"Maude, just look at this glorious day!" I exclaimed, breathing in the salty sea air. "I can practically feel my stress melting away already."

"Indeed, Mabel," she agreed, shielding her eyes from the sun with one hand. "But we didn't come here just to soak up the sun – let's get those boogie boards and hit the water!"

I stopped in my tracks as Maude trekked on. Boogie boards? What did she have in store for me and my old bones?

She paused and turned to find me, waving me toward her. Would she let me get away with just watching her? I had never done anything like this. My kids back home wouldn't believe it, even with pictures. Oh, boy!

We made our way over to the beach rental shack, its weathered wooden walls adorned with colorful signs advertising everything from surf lessons to sunblock. A young man with sun-bleached hair and a friendly grin greeted us as we approached.

"Welcome to Surf's Up Rentals! How can I help you lovely ladies today?" he asked, leaning casually against the counter.

"Two boogie boards, please," Maude replied, her eyes scanning the assortment of boards propped up against the wall.

"Coming right up!" he said, selecting two boards that he deemed suitable for our adventure. "That'll be twenty dollars, please."

Handing him a twenty and a ten, Maude said with a warm smile, "Here you are, dear. Keep the change."

"Thanks, ma'am!" he exclaimed, his face lighting up with genuine gratitude. "You two have fun out there!"

"Thank you, we will," Maude replied, taking her board with a determined gleam in her eye. "Come on, Mabel — let's show these waves who's boss."

As we entered the water, the refreshing coolness washing over our feet, I couldn't help but feel a little nervous. I had never tried boogie boarding before, and the prospect of being tossed around by the waves was daunting.

"Maude, are you sure about this?" I asked hesitantly, clutching my board with white-knuckled fingers.

"Of course! It's quite simple once you get the hang of it," she assured me, her confidence contagious. "I'll give you a quick tutorial, and you'll be riding the waves like a pro in no time."

True to her word, Maude began showing the basics of boogie boarding – how to position myself on the board, how to paddle out into the surf, and, most importantly, how to catch a wave.

"Remember, Mabel, timing is key!" she called out as she expertly rode a small wave back to shore. "Wait for the right moment to push off and let the wave do the rest!"

"Alright," I said, steeling myself for the task at hand. "Here goes nothing!"

As I waded deeper into the water, I couldn't help but marvel at the sheer joy of it all – the sun on my face, the salt on my lips, and the thrill of trying something new. With each wave that passed, my confidence grew, fueled by Maude's unwavering faith in my abilities.

I took a deep breath, my heart pounding in anticipation as I prepared to ride the waves for the first time. Maude flashed me an encouraging grin.

"Remember, Mabel, it's all about balance and timing," she reminded me, her voice barely audible over the crash of the surf.

"Right, balance and timing," I muttered to myself, gripping the edges of the boogie board tightly.

With slightly trembling hands, I positioned myself on the board just as Maude had shown me, and then paddled out into the breaking waves. The water was chilly but invigorating against my skin, and I couldn't help but feel a surge of adrenaline as I glided across the surface.

"Here comes a good one!" Maude called out, pointing to an approaching wave.

"OK, Mabel, you've got this," I whispered under my breath. I watched the wave approach, and when the moment felt right, I gave a firm push off the sandy bottom with my feet.

For a split second, everything seemed perfect. The wave caught my board, propelling me forward with a thrilling rush of speed. But then, in a blink of an eye, I lost my balance and found myself engulfed by the foamy white wave.

"Whoa!" I yelped, sputtering as I emerged from the water, soaked from head to toe. My hair clung to my face, and I wiped the salty water from my eyes.

"Ha! That was quite a ride!" Maude chuckled, her laughter warm and infectious, as she swam up beside me. "But don't worry, it happens to everyone their first time."

"Really?" I asked, unable to suppress a giggle of my own. "Well, that was definitely more fun than I expected!"

"See? I told you you'd love it," Maude said, grinning from ear to ear. "Now, let's catch some more waves!"

For the next hour or so, Maude and I continued to boogie board, reveling in the sun and the surf. Each time I managed to ride a wave without wiping out, my confidence grew, and I eagerly paddled back out for more.

As we frolicked among the gentle swells, I couldn't help but marvel at the sheer joy of it all. "Maude, this is incredible!" I shouted, breathless after catching a particularly long wave.

"Nothing like a bit of adventure to keep us young, right Mabel?" she replied with a wink.

"Absolutely!" I agreed, laughing as another wave knocked me off balance, sending me tumbling into the water once more.

And somehow, amidst the laughter and the splashing, the worries of our investigation seemed to fade away, if only for a little while.

CHAPTER SIX

As we trudged back to the car, still dripping wet from our ocean escapades, my attention was drawn to a nearby lamppost. A colorful sign, emblazoned with bold letters, shouted its protest for all to see: "NO MORE DEVELOPMENT! SAVE CRYSTAL BEACH!" While we'd been boogie boarding and laughing like schoolgirls, the number of anti-development signs had multiplied like rabbits.

"Maude, look at this," I said, nodding toward the lamppost. "It seems this little beach community is getting even more riled up."

"Indeed," Maude replied, squinting through her salt-speckled glasses as she surveyed the ever-growing forest of signs. "I've got a feeling that our suspicions about this developer are spot on.

We climbed into the car, and as we drove toward the cottage, the signs became even more numerous, their messages growing bolder and angrier with each passing block. The locals would not take this development lying down — and neither were we.

"Maude, we need a plan," I declared, my voice full of determination. "We need to figure out what's really going on here and how it ties into Kenneth's murder."

"Agreed," Maude said, her eyes narrowing in thought. "First things first, though – we need to find out who's behind these signs. They might have information that could help us."

"Right," I nodded, my mind racing with questions. "But how do we find them? Surely they won't just come forward if we ask around."

"Leave that to me," Maude replied, a mischievous glint in her eye. "I may be retired from cybersecurity, but I've still got a few tricks up my sleeve."

As we pulled into the driveway of our cozy cottage, I couldn't help but feel a renewed sense of purpose. This mystery was only getting deeper, and it was up to us to unravel it.

"Maude," I said, turning to face her as we stepped out of the car, "I don't know what you have planned, but I'm in. Whatever it takes to sort this out, we're going to do it together."

"Of course, Mabel," Maude replied. "That's what best friends are for."

And with that, we closed the car doors behind us and strode toward the cottage, our resolve stronger than ever. We may have been soaking wet and tired from an afternoon in the surf, but we were ready to dive headfirst into the swirling waters of conspiracy and intrigue that awaited us. I was right. Taking a break from the investigation had spurred us on with new ideas.

"I couldn't be more hungry. Ideas for dinner?" I asked.

We dropped our wet and sandy towels in the laundry room. "I could go for more barbecue at The Saucy Piglet. What do you think?"

Was she hoping to run into the cowboy we had seen the day before? Stan had said he would be at the next mystery club meeting. Would this encounter draw Maude back to Port la Pena for good? Going along with her, I said, "Sounds good."

As we approached the restaurant, the smell of garlic and sizzling bacon mingled with the salty sea breeze, making my stomach growl in anticipation.

"Can't wait for those bacon-wrapped shrimp!" I exclaimed, rubbing my hands together gleefully.

"Neither can I," Maude agreed. Was she more excited for the barbecue or who we might run into?

We pushed open the door and were immediately enveloped by the bustling atmosphere. It was significantly busier than our previous visit. The sounds of laughter, clinking glasses, and spirited conversations filled the air like lively music. I don't know how I missed the baffling decor before. They adorned the colorful walls with eclectic pig-themed art that ranged from the whimsical to the downright bizarre.

"Look at that!" I pointed to a painting of a pig wearing a top hat and monocle, riding a unicycle across a tightrope.

"Table for two?" A cheerful hostess asked, snapping me out of my reverie.

"Absolutely!" I replied, following her as she led us to a table nestled in a corner. As we settled into our seats, I felt a renewed sense of determination.

"Look at these salt and pepper shakers," Maude said, picking up two tiny pigs dressed in ruffled aprons. "This place is just brimming with character."

"Isn't it?" I agreed, my eyes scanning the room before returning to our conversation about Kenneth's murder. "Now, back to the matter at hand. Marty mentioned something about a proposed development. What do you make of that?"

Maude tapped her fingers on the table, deep in thought. "It's hard to say without more information, but it could be significant. Perhaps there was something underhanded going on with the developer, and Kenneth got caught in the crossfire."

"Or maybe Kenneth discovered some dirty dealings and was killed to keep him quiet," I added, sipping my water.

"Exactly." Maude nodded, her eyes narrowing. "I wonder if Marty knows more about the developer than he let on. He seemed a bit... cagey when we asked him about it."

"True." I leaned in closer, lowering my voice conspiratorially. "Do you think we should pay him another visit? Maybe we can get more information out of him about this mysterious developer."

"Definitely worth considering," Maude agreed. "But first, let's focus on finding out more about the development itself. There must be someone in town who knows what's going on."

We placed our orders as my stomach grumbled in anticipation of the delectable food. I might just have to place a to-go order to have some leftovers later.

Maude pulled out her phone and furiously tapped in a message. She took a long swig of water and returned to her phone. I expected she was connecting with a former colleague to set them on a path of discovery for the development. Setting her phone on the table, she sat back as the waitress brought our mugs of beer.

I closed my eyes and drank a sip of my beer. Oh, that hit the spot. Following that up with another, I said, "We don't know exactly what Kenneth knew, or even how he found out about it. We'll need to tread carefully here."

"Of course," she agreed, raising her mug and clinking it against mine.

As the conversation continued, I noticed Maude's gaze wandering towards the window. Her brow furrowed, and I could practically see the gears turning in her head. "What's troubling you?" I asked softly, placing a hand on her arm.

"I'm just worried about Nathan," she confessed, her eyes clouded with concern. "The police have already visited him a second time. I'm concerned that they think he did this. And if we don't act fast to find the actual killer..." Her voice trailed off.

"We'll just have to make sure we solve this mystery quickly and efficiently. The sooner we put this case to rest, the less chance there is of Nathan getting mixed up in it."

"Agreed," Maude nodded resolutely.

The waitress delivered our steaming plates of bacon wrapped shrimp. I nibbled my first bite, with a plan to find a similar recipe to make this at home.

"Alright, let's think this through," I said, wiping my mouth with a napkin. "How could the development be connected to Kenneth's murder? We need some solid theories."

Maude thought for a moment, tapping her finger against her chin. "Well," she began, "it's possible that someone else in the neighborhood didn't want the development to go forward, and they saw Kenneth's involvement as a threat."

"Or maybe," I chimed in, "someone from the development company had a personal vendetta against Kenneth. Maybe his death wasn't just about the project, but something more personal."

"True," Maude nodded. "We can't rule anything out at this stage. But we should definitely focus our efforts on finding out more about the people involved in the development and any potential conflicts of interest."

Silently, we plowed through our meals. I put a hand over my bulging stomach, wishing I had room for one of their delectable looking desserts.

"Maude, we need a plan to get more information from Kenneth's neighbors," I said, as the waitress removed our empty plates. "They might know something they haven't shared with the police."

She pulled out her phone again, typing and scrolling. I watched as those silver curls bobbed up and down, belying the fact that she was probably more tech-savvy than most people half her age. "Look here," she said, holding out her phone to me. "An open house in the neighborhood tomorrow afternoon at 2 pm – just a few houses down from Kenneth's." Her eyes gleamed with determination.

"Good idea. We can pose as potential buyers. That way, we'll have an excuse to talk to them without raising suspicion." Our plan was shaping up. Who would suspect two little old ladies were on the case to solve a murder? Whenever we grannied it up, people talked a blue streak, never realizing we were investigating. Our age was our superpower.

Maude craned her neck, scanning the room.

"I don't think he's here," I said.

She snapped her head toward me, her face red. "What?"

My friend was smitten.

Pulling her water glass toward her, she twirled it in the wet ring left on the table. The volume of the music increased as more couples made their way to the dance floor. What a fun place this was. Maude quickly glanced back as the couples swayed to the sounds. I really wished I had met her husband. I bet he was wonderful.

"OK. Back to the task at hand," she said, her game face returning. "Before we head over there tomorrow, we need a backstory for who we are and why we're looking to buy a home there."

Nodding, I said, "Good point. We may not want to reveal that we know Nathan. That might taint any conversation we might have with his neighbors."

"Sounds like a plan," Maude agreed, signaling for the check.

Our visit to Port la Pena to see Nathan and Mollie had taken quite a left turn. Not only was there a murder, but Nathan was likely considered a suspect. I hoped with all my heart that we could get him out of this, but it might not happen unless we solved the mystery. What would Maude be able to get from her cyber buddies on the developers? And would that provide any clues to who might have done this and how the new development could be connected to Kenneth's murder?

As we left The Saucy Piglet, I felt a mixture of excitement and apprehension at the prospect of questioning potential suspects, one who could be a murderer. We got into Maude's car without a word. So much had happened in a short amount of time. She slowly pulled out of the parking spot for our return trip to our cottage.

"I'm going to sleep well tonight, after that boogie boarding." I chuckled. Who says life is over at eighty? "Though I might be so sore I can't get out of bed in the morning." That was' OK. Sore muscles would provide me with a lovely memory of my time with Maude. I was still not sure how she convinced me to get out of my comfort zone, but I was glad she did.

CHAPTER SEVEN

"Maude, I'm not sure we should be here," I whispered as we parked the car outside the open house, feeling a sense of foreboding. The house stood in stark contrast to Kenneth's rundown property nearby.

"Relax, Mabel," she replied calmly, her analytical mind ticking away like a finely tuned machine. "We're just two innocent old ladies attending an open house. Nothing suspicious about that."

"Speak for yourself," I muttered under my breath. Innocent wasn't a word that had ever been used to describe me. Still, we had a mission to gather information about potential suspects in Kenneth's murder, and fear couldn't get the best of us.

As we approached the open house, the tension in the air was palpable. The stream of strangers parading through the front door seemed like vultures, gawking and gossiping.

Maude patted my shoulder, her wrinkled face creasing into a smile. "Don't you worry. We've got this."

With cautious steps, we crossed the threshold into the house, our eyes scanning the room for any signs of danger. The voices of prospective buyers filled the air, excitedly discussing granite counter tops and hardwood floors. We entered the great room with a vaulted ceiling and large glass sliding doors leading to a large yard beyond a deck. The crowd of lookers had congregated here for the time being. Maude motioned to join her near the fireplace. We angled our bodies toward each other so it wouldn't be obvious that we were here to snoop and eavesdrop.

"This is a lovely home," I bellowed as I scanned the group. How did one pick out a murderer from a crowd? And was the killer even here?

"It is, isn't it?" an older, dapper gentleman replied, approaching the built-in bookcases along the wall. "Are you looking to buy?" He looked back and forth between Maude and me. I wondered what he was thinking about two elderly women coming to an open house.

"Maybe," Maude said, reaching her hand out to shake his. "I'm Maude. This is my friend Mabel." She gestured toward me. I gave a little wave of my hand. "How about you?"

"Well, it's possible. I actually live in the neighborhood, so this might be an investment property." He ran his hand along a shelf. Looking up, he said, "I'm Blake."

We had a live wire on our hands. How could we pepper him with questions without being obvious for our intent?

Right on cue, Maude expertly offered a rationale for us to probe further. "My son Nathan and his wife live in the neighborhood." Maude pointed in the general direction of Nathan's house. "It might be nice to live a little closer to them."

"Oh, I know Nathan and Mollie. Nice couple," Blake said.

People continued to come and go in the great room. I wasn't sure how much longer we could retain Blake with questions before our intent became obvious.

Maude stepped forward with her hand to the side of her mouth. Just above a whisper, she said, "Well, thankfully, that nuisance Kenneth is gone. Not that I..." Maude held up both hands to show she had no interest in Kenneth's demise.

"You and me both, Maude. Nuisance is a generous description. That guy scammed me out of a lot of money. But it seems like Kenneth's luck finally ran out. Karma's a real pain in the behind." The web of deception woven by Kenneth had ensnared more than just us. "I think he was selling his house to skip town from everything he got from his neighbors," Blake replied bitterly, his voice filled with resentment. He stepped back, seeming to realize he had raised his voice and perhaps said too much. The crowd had quieted and looked in our direction.

"Maybe we should keep looking through the house, Maude," I said, tugging her elbow. Had we just met a killer face-to-face? Blake was angry enough and had a motive. When you messed with someone's money, they rarely took kindly to that.

"Yes. Nice to meet you, Blake," Maude said, sweetness dripping from her voice.

We walked arm-in-arm down the hallway. I glanced in the first room to our right, dipping in there with Maude and closing the door. Breathlessly, I said, "What do you think?"

Maude nodded. "Could be, Mabel. But I think we've just gotten started." She pulled out her phone and quickly typed in a message. No doubt a request to her cyber pals for some background on Blake. If he was looking for investment properties, was he in on the new development coming to the town?

I stepped away from the door and looked around the room. We had entered a den that looked like it was used for an office. I peeked out the window to see several people milling around on the back lawn. The more we explored, the more convoluted this mystery became.

Maude's phone buzzed, and she started typing a reply.

Wandering around the room to catch my breath. "Look at this," I called out, gesturing to a photo album tucked away on a bookshelf. The pages revealed snapshots of Kenneth at various social events, always surrounded by an ever-changing cast of characters. Some faces appeared more frequently than others - potential suspects, perhaps?

"Interesting," Maude mused, her brow furrowed in concentration. She took several snaps of the photos. "Why don't we see if any of these people are here today? They might shed some light on our investigation."

"Good idea," I replied, feeling a renewed sense of determination. We split up, each armed with a mental list of names and faces to track down. As I meandered through the crowded rooms, making small talk and discreetly probing for information, I couldn't help but notice the undercurrent of tension that seemed to permeate the atmosphere. It was as if everyone here was hiding something, and it was up to us to uncover their secrets.

Maude appeared at my side, her eyes wide with excitement. She nudged me and pointed towards a group of people huddled together in the corner of the great room. "Listen," she whispered, her usually booming voice barely audible. I strained my ears, catching snippets of their conversation.

"Such a shame about Kenneth's home," one woman sighed, shaking her head with a disapproving cluck. "It's an eyesore, really."

"Hello, folks!" I chimed in, trying to sound as casual as possible while inching towards them. "Terrible business about Kenneth, wasn't it? Such a tragedy." The group nodded in agreement, and Maude and I exchanged knowing glances, silently urging each other to dig deeper.

"Speaking of tragedies," I continued, "it's such a pity that Kenneth's property has become so neglected. Has anyone else noticed that?"

"Absolutely," the woman replied, clearly eager to share her thoughts. "His garden is practically a jungle! And to think that we have to live next door to that mess…"

All heads in the circle nodded in unison. Seems Kenneth didn't have many friends in the neighborhood, despite the photos to the contrary. Had they all been chummy at one time before things took a turn?

This investigative field trip was providing quite a list of possibilities to investigate.

Just then, the slider from the back deck opened and a woman strode inside, surveying the room with a practiced eye. She was tall and thin as a rail, dressed in a crisp pantsuit and heels that clicked sharply against the hardwood floor. A golden name tag gleamed on her lapel, identifying her as the real estate agent: "Samantha Greene."

"Welcome!" Samantha called in a booming voice as she approached us with an outstretched hand. "I'm Samantha, the agent for this lovely property. So glad to see so many of you here today." She handed her business card to the couple that had followed her inside from the back. Leaning in she whispered to them and pointed to the kitchen.

I exchanged a glance with Maude, eyes glinting with amusement. After introducing ourselves as "just browsing," we listened with feigned interest as Samantha launched into her well-rehearsed sales pitch, touting the home's "charming" features and "ideal location."

"The housing market in this area is extremely competitive, you know," Samantha said in a conspiratorial tone. "Properties like this don't come along often. I have several other clients eager to make an offer, so if you're seriously interested, you'll need to act fast."

I stifled a snort. Samantha had "several other clients" and a bridge in Brooklyn to sell us too, no doubt. Her transparent tactics might work on some, but Maude and I were not so easily fooled.

Still, we asked a few questions about the neighborhood and nearby amenities, hoping to glean some useful information from Samantha's chatter. Maude's gaze remained sharp, analyzing the agent's every word and gesture for signs of deceit or evasion.

"What about that other house for sale down the street?" I asked Samantha.

Her chin dipped, and she said through gritted teeth, "I'm not the representative for that dump."

"Oh, do you know who is?" Maude asked sweetly, knowing full well that it was Gina.

Brushing down the front of her pantsuit, Samantha continued, "It should have been me."

Was this just some friendly competition between professionals, or was there something deeper going on in the real estate business in Port la Pena?

After a few minutes, Maude glanced at her watch and sighed. "Well, it seems we have taken up enough of your time. Thank you for the tour, Ms. Greene, but I'm afraid this property is not quite what we had in mind."

Samantha's polite smile strained at the edges, her annoyance clear. But she recovered quickly, extending another hand to shake. "Completely understandable. It was a pleasure meeting you both. Please keep my card in case you have questions about homes in this area."

We bid Samantha goodbye and headed for the exit, the click of her heels fading behind us. Out on the front steps, Maude frowned pensively at the "For Sale" sign.

"Not the most trustworthy sort, that one," she mused. "I wonder what else she might be selling besides houses."

"Skeletons in closets?" I suggested. "Dark secrets?"

"Indeed." Maude's eyes gleamed knowingly. "I have a feeling Samantha Greene's involvement in this mystery has only just begun."

Maude and I silently strode to our car, pondering the experience we just had. It was possible we had just met a killer, but then again, maybe none of the neighbors had anything to do with Kenneth's death.

Stopping at the driver's door, Maude halted and looked at me across the roof of the car. She glanced around to see who else might be observing us. Leaning in, she said, "I have an idea." She pulled out her phone and quickly tapped in a message. That thing was our lifeline to details we probably weren't even supposed to have from her former cybersecurity colleagues. With one more look, she gestured for me to follow her.

Maude made a beeline down the sidewalk, straight to the path leading to Kenneth's front door. She looked at her phone as it buzzed. "Got it." I followed her as she approached the lockbox hanging on the water faucet to the right of the front door. Were we really just about to break into Kenneth's house? If we got caught, we might just launch ourselves into first place for prime suspects of his murder. Don't criminals usually return to the scene of the crime? This could either make or break us. She quickly punched in the code from her phone and retrieved the keys. Swiftly stepping to the front door, she unlocked it, and we slid inside.

"Are you crazy?" I said. "This is one of the riskiest things we've ever done to solve a case."

I knew Maude would stop at nothing to solve this and make sure that Nathan was in the clear. The mustiness from our prior visit lingered in the air, now combined with the metallic smell of dried blood.

CHAPTER EIGHT

"Good heavens, did he ever clean up?" I muttered, trying not to gag at the sight and smell of empty fast food containers strewn about. The floor was a minefield of greasy wrappers and discarded soda cups. I wrinkled my nose, careful not to step on anything that might give away our presence.

"Clearly not," Maude said, navigating the mess with surprising agility. "You know what they say: "You can't take the trash out of the man.""

"Or the man out of the trash, apparently." I shook my head at the sad state of affairs. Poor Kenneth. His life had become such a mess before it had been so abruptly snuffed out.

"Let's not waste any time. We need to gather as much information as possible before someone discovers us here," Maude urged, the determination in her eyes reminding me why I admired her so much.

"Right you are." I nodded, steeling myself for the task at hand. We had a murder to solve, and this filthy hallway might just hold the key to unlocking the truth about Kenneth's untimely demise.

Pressing further into the darkened house, we quickly skirted past the room where Kenneth's body had been found. I shuddered involuntarily at the memory of his lifeless form sprawled on the floor, a grim reminder of our purpose here. Maude caught my eye and gave me a reassuring nod; even in the face of danger, her unwavering bravery was contagious.

"His office should be just around the corner if it's laid out similarly to Nathan and Mollie's," she whispered, leading the way.

"Let's hope it isn't as messy as the rest of the house," I muttered under my breath, still trying to shake off the unsettling feeling that clung to the air like a fog.

But alas, as we entered the room, my hopes were dashed. Papers upon papers were stacked haphazardly on every surface, with some spilling onto the floor like a papery waterfall. I couldn't help but wonder if Kenneth had a filing system known only to himself, or if he simply reveled in chaos.

"Wow," I said, taking in the disarray. "It's like a tornado tore through an office supply store."

"Focus, Mabel," Maude chided gently. "We need to find anything that might point us in the right direction."

"Right, right." I rolled up my sleeves and approached the nearest stack of papers, trying not to disturb the delicate balance they seemed to have achieved. "Who knew one man could accumulate so much... stuff?"

"Stuff" seemed like the most appropriate word given the situation, but I couldn't help but feel a twinge of sympathy for Kenneth. Even in death, his secrets were laid bare for all to see — or, at least, for two intrepid amateur sleuths to uncover.

As we sifted through the mountains of documents, I could tell that Maude was growing increasingly frustrated. Her brow furrowed. She muttered something under her breath that sounded suspiciously like a curse.

"Any luck?" I ventured, trying to suppress a sigh as I abandoned yet another stack of seemingly irrelevant papers.

"Nothing yet," she grumbled, tossing a crumpled sheet back onto the desk. "But we can't give up." She tiptoed around the room. "Look at this." she exclaimed, holding up a foreclosure notice with a dramatic flourish. "Dated two months ago. Poor Kenneth was about to lose his house."

"Yikes," I said sympathetically, though I couldn't help but wonder whether Kenneth's financial woes had played a part in his untimely demise. "It seems he was drowning in debt. Here are bank statements showing an overdrawn balance of over $10,000."

Maude's eyes widened as she scanned the numbers, her lips pursed in an almost comically exaggerated frown. "I suppose even scammers can fall on hard times," she mused, her tone both pitying and disdainful. "But it makes one wonder what else he was mixed up in."

"Speaking of which," I interjected, holding up a cardboard tube I'd found tucked away behind a teetering pile of paperbacks, "look at these." I carefully extracted the rolled-up documents from their cylindrical home, revealing detailed drawings of the waterfront development that had been causing such a stir in our little town.

"By George, you've got something there!" she cried, her earlier frustration momentarily forgotten in the face of our latest discovery. "And would you look at that –" she pointed at the name printed neatly in the corner of the plans, "– Samantha Greene, the city planner who approved the project. Interesting."

"Very interesting," I agreed. My mind raced to piece together the potential connections between Kenneth's debts, his real estate schemes, and his unfortunate end. "Do you think Samantha Greene knew about Kenneth's financial troubles? Could she have had a hand in his murder?"

"Perhaps," Maude said, her steely gaze fixed on the documents as though trying to will them to reveal their secrets. "Or perhaps not. But one thing is for certain –" she looked up at me, her eyes glittering with determination, "– we won't rest until we've found the truth."

I looked at my watch. By my calculation, we had been inside about ten minutes. Before we began living on borrowed time, we needed to quickly finish. Was any of what we discovered enough by itself to implicate Samantha?

"Let's see what else we can find in this mess. But we have to hurry," I suggested, eyeing the precarious stacks of paper teetering on Kenneth's desk. As I began sifting through the documents, Maude continued her inspection of the cluttered office.

"Ah-ha!" she exclaimed triumphantly, plucking a sheet from the disarray. She brandished it in my direction like a conquistador wielding a newly discovered treasure map. "Look at this."

I squinted at the paper, noting the bold header: "'Contract — VOID.'" Below, I spotted Blake Stevens' name and signature. My eyebrows shot up like two surprised caterpillars taking flight.

"Blake? The real estate developer who's been pushing for the waterfront development?" I asked.

"Indeed," Maude confirmed, her eyes narrowing with suspicion. "It seems he had some sort of agreement with Kenneth, but it was declared void. I wonder if Kenneth backed out, leaving Blake high and dry?"

"Maybe that's why Blake was so angry at him," I mused, feeling the gears of my mind whirring to life. "But what about Samantha Greene? How does she fit into all of this?"

As we continued our search, I noticed Kenneth's computer, which hummed quietly in the corner. Maude must have had the same thought as she approached the machine with the determination of a cat stalking its prey.

"Perhaps we can find more information on here," she said, settling into the chair in front of the computer. Her slender fingers hovered over the keyboard as she attempted to log in.

"Password-protected, of course," she muttered under her breath, the corners of her mouth turning down in frustration. "We're going to have to leave this for a return visit."

Relieved that we were wrapping up, I agreed. We had gathered more pieces to the puzzle, but what picture was it beginning to reveal?

The moment we stepped back into the hallway, the suffocating smell of stale fast food immediately struck me. It appeared every greasy burger and limp fry Kenneth had ever consumed had lingered in the air, smothering us with its unwelcome presence.

"Ugh, you can practically taste the cholesterol," I muttered, wrinkling my nose.

"Good thing we're not staying for dinner," Maude quipped, her voice muffled by the scarf she'd wrapped around her face like a bandit.

"Ah, Maude and Mabel! Just in time for our mystery club meeting," Erin said with a bright smile, her eyes sparkling with anticipation. "We have quite the crowd today, so I've set up the back room for us."

"Lead the way," Maude replied.

"Did you both have a nice day?" Erin asked as she led us through the narrow aisles of books, her snug jeans topping another cute pair of cowgirl boots.

Maude and I whipped our heads toward each other behind Erin's back. Nice didn't exactly describe the state of affairs that we found at Kenneth's. "It was certainly an adventure," I said.

"Here we are," Erin announced, pushing open a creaky door to reveal a cozy room filled with overstuffed armchairs and a large wooden table piled high with books. The walls were lined with shelves overflowing with every mystery novel imaginable, and the soft glow of lamplight cast flickering shadows on the floor.

"Ah, Maude, Mabel! Delightful to see you again," Stan said, adjusting his glasses with one hand and extending the other for a handshake. "Always a pleasure."

"Likewise, Stan," Maude replied, accepting his handshake with a lingering look in her eye.

Before we could get comfortable in our seats, the door swung open, and in sauntered three more club members. We made introductions all around as we met Jack, Gabi, and London.

Settling into our seats, we began chatting about our recent trip to the beach. "I couldn't believe the commotion," I started, pausing for dramatic effect. "The whole town is in an uproar about the new proposed development."

"Yes, it's supposed to be condos." Jack shook his head. "A monstrosity of glass and steel that would loom over the quaint seaside cottages like a hungry beast."

"Such a shame," Gabi sighed, shaking her head. "It's always the little people who suffer most."

Rubbing his hands together, Stan said, "Where should we start today?" His smile gleamed toward Maude.

"Well," Maude jumped up from her seat and paced the length of the table. She had an audience. The room fell silent, the air thick with anticipation. "We have a real-life mystery to solve." She inhaled deeply. I watched the pain on her face, not realizing until this moment just how stressful this had been for her. Investigating one of her own family.

"Go on," London urged, her eyes alight with intrigue.

The door opened with a squeak, and we all jumped. Erin re-entered the room, looking around at the stoic faces all geared toward Maude. She quietly took a seat next to London, her notepad in front of her.

"Maude's son Nathan had a neighbor named Kenneth," I explained, my voice wavering slightly as I recalled the grisly details. "He was murdered, and because Nathan had a restraining order against him, he's become a suspect in the case."

"Good heavens!" Gabi gasped, her hand flying to her mouth in shock.

"Surely they don't believe Nathan could do such a thing," Jack said, his brow furrowing with concern.

"Of course not," Maude huffed indignantly, "but we must clear his name and find the real culprit. I assure you, there is no shortage of suspects in this sordid tale."

How far was she going to go to reveal our sleuthing?

Maude rose again, her energy propelling her around the table. "Let me share with you the information we've gathered so far," she began, her voice steady and determined. "Kenneth was killed in his own home on Tuesday evening between 8:15 and 9:00 PM. The murder weapon seems to be a blunt object."

"Maude and I have done a bit of... investigating," I continued hesitantly, "and uncovered some interesting details. There's one neighbor, Blake Stevens, who lost a considerable amount of money to Kenneth in a shady business deal. Then there's Samantha Greene, a real estate agent and rival to Gina – the woman Kenneth was last seen with before his untimely demise."

"Where did you find this information?" Jack inquired, raising an eyebrow.

"Never you mind," I replied, unwilling to disclose our methods. "Suffice it to say, we have reason to believe these people might have had a motive."

Maude resumed her seat, looking at everyone seated at the table. "Would you be interested in helping to solve this case?"

CHAPTER NINE

"Would we?" Stan began. "Just try to stop us!"

Erin put her laptop on the table. "How about I get us set up with a new folder on the forum? You never know if others around the world just might have some insights we might miss." She pulled her cute glasses from her head and bent over the laptop.

"Yeah. Remember that case of the cows that were dropping dead on old Tommy's farm?" London asked. All heads nodded. "It took a chemical engineer from France to suggest a connection for us to follow."

I was convinced we need our own Book Nook mystery forum back home. This just sealed the deal.

"Thank you, everyone," Maude whispered.

"Perhaps we should consider those who were opposed to Kenneth's proposed development project," suggested Gabi. "There must have been residents and businesses in the beach town who were furious about it."

"Excellent point," agreed Maude, her eyes narrowing as she pondered the implications. "They might have seen Kenneth as a threat to their way of life and taken matters into their own hands."

"Actually," interjected London, the true crime aficionado, "I heard rumors about an outspoken environmental activist who was campaigning against the development. Her name is Carly Waters, and she was trying to rally support to save the shoreline. Could be worth looking into."

"Interesting," I mused, scribbling down the information on a scrap of paper. "An eco-warrior with a motive to protect her beloved environment at any cost? I like it."

Erin furiously typed as we talked.

"Oh," Maude said, pulling out her phone and raising it in the air. "I forgot I took some pics of the protesters." She scrolled through her phone, tapping it several times. Erin gave her the website address to upload the pictures to the forum folder.

For the first time, I felt confident we would actually find the killer. But would it be before Nathan got arrested? Did the police even have any other suspects? Erin expertly walked us through all the details we had gathered and loaded them into our forum folder. The group quizzed us up one side and down the other for any other information. With their individual expertise, they each contributed theories along with their knowledge of what was happening with the development that was affecting their neighborhoods.

"Thank you again for including us in this, Maude," Jack said. "We're here to help in any way we can. They won't get away with it."

A lump formed in my throat at the outpouring of support from our new friends. My eyes stung, and I had to blink rapidly to avoid tearing up. "You're all so kind," I managed to say. "It means the world to me — to us. With your help, we'll get to the bottom of this."

"Here, here!" Jack raised his coffee mug in a toast. We all followed suit.

The mystery club was officially on the case. Kenneth Andrews' killer didn't stand a chance.

Maude and I left the Book Nook in high spirits, our minds racing with new clues and suspects to investigate. The chill autumn air felt refreshing after the cozy warmth of the bookstore.

"Can you believe how eager they all are to help?" Maude said, looping her arm through mine. Her eyes sparkled behind her bifocals, as bright as the stars emerging in the deepening twilight.

"Maude," I mused aloud, "do you think we're on the right track with this eco-warrior angle?"

She shrugged as we approached our car. "Not sure. But the more we can rule people out, the closer we'll be to finding the killer."

"Rise and shine, Mabel!" Maude's voice pierced through my still-drowsy mind like a shot of espresso. I blinked open my eyes to see her standing at the foot of my bed, fully dressed and raring to go.

"Ugh, morning already?" I groaned, rubbing sleep from my eyes with the back of my hand.

"Morning indeed, my friend! We've got a mystery to solve, remember? Kenneth Andrews isn't going to un-murder himself, and we need to clear Nathan's name," she said with an infectious enthusiasm that was near impossible to resist.

"Alright, alright, I'm up," I muttered, swinging my legs over the side of the bed. The thought of Nathan being wrongly accused sent a shiver down my spine, even in the warmth of my sunlit bedroom.

I quickly got ready as we left the cottage for a stop at The Pecan Patch for some pastries on our way to Nathan's. Maude wanted to check on him and Mollie.

As we approached Nathan's, I noticed a younger woman standing at Kenneth's front door, fumbling with a set of keys. This was certainly an unexpected sight.

"Maude, who do you think that is?" I whispered, trying to keep my voice low as we neared Nathan's front porch.

"Couldn't say, but she must be important if she has a key to Kenneth's house," Maude replied, her eyes narrowing with suspicion. "Let's not draw attention to ourselves just yet."

"Good plan."

As we entered Nathan's living room, we found him pacing back and forth, his brow furrowed in worry. He looked like a man who hadn't slept in days, and I couldn't help but feel a pang of sympathy for him.

"Mom, Mabel, I'm glad you're here," Nathan said, his voice strained. "I've been going out of my mind thinking about all this. What if they arrest me for Kenneth's murder?"

"Relax, dear," Maude said soothingly, crossing the room to place a comforting hand on his arm. "We know you had nothing to do with it, and we're going to prove it."

"Exactly," I chimed in, hoping to bolster his spirits. "Besides, we saw someone entering Kenneth's house just now. It could be a lead."

"Really?" Nathan asked, his face lighting up with a glimmer of hope. "Who was it?"

"We don't know yet," Maude admitted, her eyes twinkling with anticipation. "But you can bet your bottom dollar we're going to find out."

"Mom, please be careful," Nathan implored, his concern for our safety touching my heart. "I don't want you two getting into any trouble on my account." He ran his hand through his hair. "Or worse, getting arrested yourselves."

Maude looked at me. I nodded.

"What?" Nathan asked, looking back and forth between us. "You know something, don't you?" He grabbed Maude's hand and pulled her to a nearby chair, standing over her. "Spill it."

I sat nearby, wondering how much she would reveal about our shenanigans. Maybe it would be best to just come clean with Nathan.

"Hi, ladies." Mollie entered the eerily quiet room.

Handing her the bag of pastries, I said, "We thought we'd bring some treats." Would that ease the conversation at all?

Maude and Nathan stared each other down. I imagined they'd had many instances of that over the years with their relationship. Neither of them was willing to blink. I briefly pondered jumping in, but decided it was not my place.

"Nathan. You know I wouldn't do anything dangerous," Maude said. Dangerous, no. But ill-advised? Uh, yes.

He stepped back and waved his arm toward the door. "I know you're itching to go check out that woman."

Maude bolted up, hugging him and kissing him on the cheek. Without a word, we left the house.

As determined as ever, we walked up to Kenneth's front door. The air carried the distant sound of laughter from children playing nearby, a stark contrast to the somber reason for our visit.

We knocked on the door and waited, the seconds ticking by like hours. Just when it appeared she wasn't going to answer, the door creaked open, revealing the young woman we'd seen earlier. She eyed us warily, her arms crossed protectively over her chest.

"Can I help you?" she asked, her tone guarded.

"Good morning," Maude cheerily said. An attempt to get more flies with honey than vinegar. "I'm Maude, and this is my good friend Mabel." I hoped two elderly ladies on the doorstep would disarm her to open up to us. "My son Nathan lives next door." Maude paused.

The woman hesitated, her gaze flitting between us before settling on me. "I'm Sarah," she finally said, her voice softening just a touch. "Sarah Andrews... Kenneth was my father."

"Ah, family ties," Maude observed, nodding sagely. "No wonder you seemed so distraught."

"Distraught?" Sarah repeated, her guard instantly back up. "Hardly. My father and I had an on-again, off-again relationship. We had just recently reconnected."

"Really?" I asked, surprised by her admission. "If you don't mind me asking, what caused the rift between you two?" Never one to mince words, I jumped to the heart of the matter, hoping she didn't slam the door right in our face.

"Life," Sarah sighed, her shoulders slumping as she leaned against the door frame. "He always had business ventures going that... well, let's just say I didn't agree with them."

Maude and I exchanged glances, our shared curiosity piqued. "Well, Sarah," Maude said, placing a comforting hand on the young woman's arm, "we'd like to help unravel the mystery of your father's death. Perhaps in doing so, we can also bring some closure for you."

"I don't know why I'm crying," Sarah murmured, tears pooling in her eyes. "It's probably mean to say, but he hurt a lot of people."

We continued to chat on the doorstep, which was just fine with me. After seeing the insides first-hand yesterday, Sarah was doing us a favor keeping us on the porch where we could at least breathe some fresh air.

"Sarah," Maude ventured, her eyes narrowing as she put on her analytical hat, "is there anyone you can think of who might have wished him harm?"

I watched Sarah's face closely, taking in the subtle tightening around her eyes and the slight quiver in her lower lip. She stared at the ground for a moment before finally looking up to meet our gazes.

"Actually," she said hesitantly, "there was one person he had a falling out with recently. A business associate named Blake. I don't know his last name."

"Blake..." I repeated. Could that be the same Blake who lived in the neighborhood and had the voided contract with Kenneth? Beside me, Maude tapped her chin thoughtfully, her eyes sparkling with determination.

"Interesting," she murmured. "And do you know what the nature of their disagreement was?"

Sarah shook her head, clearly frustrated. "Not exactly. Dad wasn't very forthcoming with information about his business dealings, mostly because he knew I didn't approve. But I overheard them arguing on the phone a few weeks ago, and it sounded pretty heated."

"Thank you, Sarah. You've been most helpful. We'll be sure to keep you informed of any developments in the case."

"Please do," Sarah nodded, her eyes filled with gratitude. "And... thank you, both of you. I didn't expect to find allies in all of this."

Maude and I stepped off the porch and headed back to Nathan's. I squeezed Maude's elbow and whispered. "Blake just shot to the top of the suspect list in my book."

Glancing around, Maude agreed. She held out her arm. "I have goosebumps." She sped up as we opened Nathan's front door to an expectant look on Nathan and Mollie's faces.

"Well?" Mollie started.

"Why don't we crack open those pastries and celebrate with some coffee," Maude said, heading to the kitchen.

Mollie followed and got out some plates and cups.

"Who was the woman?" Nathan asked.

"That was Kenneth's daughter. I think we have a better idea of what might have happened." Maude said, seating herself at the table.

"Please let the police know and have them take over. Mom, I'm very concerned about you and Mabel."

"He's right, Maude," I said. Mollie dished everyone a pastry and a cup of coffee. "If someone knows we're homing in on the killer, they might get scared, and this could turn out even worse."

Maude munched her pastry as she nodded and licked the cinnamon sugar from her fingers. "Yes, I agree." Nobody in the room believed for a minute that she would stop looking.

CHAPTER TEN

"Maude, are you sure this is wise?" I asked as we left Nathan's home, the sun-cast shadows stretching out on the sidewalk before us.

"Absolutely!" Maude replied with her signature determination, her curly gray hair bobbing as she strode toward our car. "We need to prove that Blake Stevens was Kenneth's killer and free Nathan from suspicion."

"Alright," I sighed, knowing there was no dissuading my dear friend once she'd set her mind on something. We climbed into our trusty old car, the worn leather seats creaking in protest as we settled in.

"Let's head toward the beach," Maude said, starting the engine. "I want to take a closer look at that new development Kenneth had been so adamant about."

We slowly drove through town, the quaint storefronts giving way to a sprawling construction site near the water. The breeze carried the scent of saltwater and earth, while skeletal frames of buildings loomed ominously above us.

"I can't believe all this land used to be part of the beach." Maude craned her neck, looking at all the new construction in process.

"Times change, I guess," I mused. "And sometimes not for the better. This whole project reeks of corruption."

We silently continued our trek through the labyrinth that would ultimately result in high-rise condos and upscale shops.

"Especially considering what we've learned about Kenneth's shady dealings," I added, thinking back to all the money he had scammed from his neighbors, including Blake Stevens. "You know, I'm thinking you might be right about Blake being involved in all this."

We continued our slow drive through town, the weight of our investigation heavy on our minds. "Let's see what other clues we can find to tie him to Kenneth's murder."

As we continued our drive, I noticed an uptick in "for sale" signs lining the streets. "Look at all these houses up for sale." My heart ached for all of those who were going to be displaced.

"Indeed," she agreed, her eyes scanning the row of neatly manicured lawns and identical white picket fences. "Seems like more and more people are being driven out by this new development."

"Or maybe they're just trying to get away from Blake before he loses it completely," I quipped, only half-joking.

"Ha! Maybe so," Maude chuckled, her eyes alight with amusement. Then she pointed to a cluster of protest signs outside a local business. "And would you look at that? Seems we're not the only ones who think something's fishy about this whole situation."

"Save Our Beach" and "No More Luxury Condos" were scrawled across the signs in bold, angry letters. We exchanged a knowing glance, our suspicions growing stronger by the minute.

"Maude, I'm famished," I declared as we cruised down Main Street. "Let's stop at that cozy little café on the corner to grab some lunch and talk about our investigation."

"Good idea, Mabel," Maude agreed, pulling into a parking spot right in front of The Whisk & Spoon.

As we entered the café, the tinkling of wind chimes greeted us, along with an inviting aroma of freshly baked bread and coffee. The lighting was soft and warm, casting a golden glow over the eclectic mix of tables and chairs scattered around the room. The place was bustling with the lunchtime crowd. The waitress seated us at a table near the back wall.

"Maude, doesn't that man look like Detective Peters?" I whispered, nodding surreptitiously in his direction.

"Wouldn't surprise me if he's keeping tabs on us," she replied with a wry grin. "But remember, Mabel, we've got nothing to hide. We're simply two law-abiding citizens who are exceptional amateur sleuths."

"True," I said, trying to suppress my irritation at the thought of being spied upon. "But it's so infuriating to be treated like suspects ourselves when we're trying to solve this case!"

The waitress arrived with our coffee as we placed our order. We smiled as she left.

"We need to focus on the evidence against Blake and how best to proceed with our investigation," Maude said.

"Right," I agreed, sitting back in my chair, clasping my hands on the table. "So far, we know Blake had a motive to kill Kenneth because of the money he lost in his scam, and we found that suspicious voided contract."

"Exactly," Maude said, dabbing her lips delicately with a napkin after sipping her coffee. "But we need more concrete evidence to convince the police – or even Detective Peters over there – that Blake is our man."

"Perhaps we should pay another visit to some of the other neighbors," I suggested. "Someone might have seen something they haven't mentioned yet."

Just as the sandwiches arrived, I spotted a familiar face entering the café. It was none other than Marty Lewis, the antique store owner with whom Maude and I had struck up a friendly rapport.

"Maude, look who's here! It's Marty," I whispered excitedly, nodding in his direction.

"Ah, our esteemed purveyor of fine antiques!" Maude exclaimed, waving him over with a flourish. "Join us for lunch."

Marty grinned and sauntered over, pulling up a chair to our table. "Hello, ladies. What a treat to see you again."

"Don't you have a store to run?" Maude asked.

"Well, yes. But as you saw when you visited the other day, the customers are fewer and farther between. I don't think a lunch break is going to doom me right now." He pointed to an item on the menu and handed it back to the waitress. Gesturing to the food in front of us, he said, "Please eat. My food will be here soon enough."

I glanced over at Detective Peters, who had angled his chair to face us. Was he actually trying to listen in to our conversation? Was he incompetent or so desperate in his investigation that he had to rely on the work of two grannies to help him out?

"I'm so glad I ran into you. Mabel, can you shed any light on a curious figurine that I discovered in my store?"

My eyes widened. Marty was outing me.

"Mabes, you didn't!" Maude said, almost spewing her food across the table. She grabbed a napkin and held it in front of her mouth while she finished chewing.

I sat up straight, proud of my creative marketing for my garden gnome business. My business partner and I had created mini-versions that had my business name on the bottom. IF somebody found it, they could go on-line to my website and order. We did fairly brisk business that way.

The waitress brought Marty's Reuben sandwich. If we returned to this café, I would order that next. It might be a gut bomb, but it looked delicious. "I think it's brilliant marketing."

"Would you like to do a wholesale order for your store?" I asked.

Marty chuckled after taking a big bite of his sandwich. He paused while he chewed it, possibly trying to think of a response that wouldn't let me down. "You know, Mabel, I'm frankly ready to try about anything to generate more business. Why not?"

Clapping my hands, I pulled a business card from my purse and handed it to him. This was turning out to be quite a productive stop.

The waitress arrived for a coffee refill and to remove our empty plates. I peeked over my cup at Maude as I sipped. We made eye contact, and she slightly nodded.

"Marty," Maude paused. She leaned in and slightly adjusted her body so she was facing away from Detective Peters.

"Yes," he said, quickly glancing at me.

Maude continued, "Marty, we've been looking into Blake Stevens's potential involvement in Kenneth's murder."

"Ah, yes. That dreadful business." Marty shuddered, rubbing his hands together as if the very mention of the murder chilled him to the bone.

"Indeed," I chimed in. "And we've found some interesting evidence that suggests he might be our guy. Blake lost a significant amount of money to Kenneth in a recent investment scam. He was furious, and we believe he would do anything to get even."

"And," Maude started. "We know there was a contract between Kenneth and Blake that was broken." I doubted she would reveal how we knew that.

"Goodness!" Marty exclaimed, his eyes widening. "That certainly sounds incriminating."

"Of course, we're not jumping to conclusions," I assured him. "It could all be a coincidence, but it's definitely worth exploring further."

Marty leaned closer to us, his brow furrowed, as if he were about to share a great secret. "Well, speaking of coincidences, I came across some rather intriguing information myself."

"Really?" Maude perked up, her eyes gleaming with curiosity.

"Yes, it turns out that Kenneth had made a rather large donation to Mayor Thompson's re-election campaign. A whopping fifty thousand dollars, if you can believe it."

"Good heavens!" I gasped, my hand flying to my chest. "But why?"

Movement from a table across the room caught my eye. Detective Peters stared in our direction. He was far enough away that I doubted he could hear, but we should keep our voices down.

Marty glanced around, as if confirming there were no eavesdroppers, before continuing in a hushed tone. "Well, our dear mayor is pushing for that commercial development on the waterfront, and Kenneth had a big stake in it. Supposedly, the mayor was promised a substantial payoff once the deal went through."

"Ahem!" Detective Peters cleared his throat loudly as he approached our table, his lunch now finished. "Ladies, Marty," he said, nodding curtly. "I couldn't help but overhear some of the conversation you were having." So much for our furtive attempt at secrecy.

Maude, ever the bold one, arched her eyebrow and replied, "And what conversation might that be, Detective?"

"About Kenneth's murder and Blake's involvement," he stated flatly, crossing his arms. "I must remind you, this is an ongoing investigation, and your meddling could jeopardize everything we've been working on."

"Meddling?" I sputtered indignantly, feeling my cheeks flush. "Detective, we're just trying to help uncover the truth!"

"Help? Ha!" Detective Peters snorted. "You listen here, all of you." He pointed at each of us in turn. "I'm narrowing down on a suspect, and if you three mess it up, you'll end up in jail just like them. So, stay out of it."

As he practically stomped away, I looked at Maude and Marty, my jaw set in determination. "Well, that was quite the warning," I muttered, tapping my fingers on the table.

"Indeed," Maude agreed, her eyes narrowed as she watched Detective Peters disappear around the corner. "But maybe he's just jealous that we've gotten more done than him on this case."

"Who knows?" Marty shrugged.

"Right," I said, clenching my fists under the table. Was Detective Peters just bloviating or did he actually have a bead on a suspect for an arrest? I squeezed my eyes shut. It couldn't be Nathan. In our short time looking into this, Maude and I found several suspects with motives. But that meant nothing if the police had narrowed their scope to Nathan.

"Alright," Maude said, her voice low and serious. "Let's go over this again: Blake had a motive to kill Kenneth because of the money he lost in the scam. We also know that Kenneth made a substantial donation to a political campaign supporting that controversial waterfront development."

I nodded emphatically. "I can't help but feel like we're missing something here, though."

Marty tapped his fingers on the table, a pensive expression on his face. "Perhaps there's another connection between Kenneth and the politician that we haven't discovered yet."

As we exchanged theories and ideas, I couldn't shake the feeling that Detective Peters' warning still hung over us like a dark cloud. What if we inadvertently sabotaged his investigation? Or worse, what if we did something that landed Nathan in jail? I shivered at the thought, trying to push it out of my mind.

"Look," Marty said, interrupting my internal turmoil. "I think we should focus on gathering more evidence first. If we find something concrete that links Blake to Kenneth's murder, we won't be stepping on anyone's toes. We'll simply be presenting the truth."

Maude nodded, her eyes gleaming with determination. "Agreed. And I think we should start by looking into the politician who received Kenneth's donation. There might be something there that could blow this entire case wide open."

"Sounds like a plan," I chimed in, feeling my spirits lift. "We'll follow the money and see where it leads us."

CHAPTER ELEVEN

"Whew, that was quite a conversation with Marty," I said as Maude and I stepped out of the cozy café, leaving our friend behind. "Never thought antique store owners would be so well-informed about murder cases."

"Neither did I," Maude agreed, her eyes twinkling with amusement. "But I suppose when your business involves digging up old treasures, you're bound to stumble upon a few secrets as well."

As we drove, the bustling business district gradually gave way to a quaint neighborhood where the new development was set to take place — Kenneth's last grand scheme before his untimely demise.

"Look at all these 'for sale' signs," Maude murmured, her brow furrowing as she maneuvered the car along the tree-lined streets. "So sad progress has to come at the expense of these lovely homes."

"Maybe Kenneth wasn't happy with just scamming the neighbors out of their money for political favors," I mused. "Perhaps he wanted their homes as well, and someone decided enough was enough."

"Or someone else had their eye on this prime real estate and didn't want Kenneth in their way," Maude added.

"Maude, do you ever miss working in cybersecurity?" I asked suddenly, my thoughts turning from the scenery to our unlikely partnership as amateur detectives.

"Sometimes," she admitted, her eyes on the road. "But there's something invigorating about solving mysteries in person, don't you think? Besides, two elderly women. What an excellent cover to chase criminals and uncover secrets."

I chuckled. We had used that to our advantage more often than not. Unsuspecting grannies feigning helplessness had gotten us pretty far in some of our investigations.

As we turned the corner onto Maple Street, I couldn't help but notice a figure standing on the sidewalk in front of a cheerful yellow Victorian house. The "For Sale" sign in the yard seemed to mock the innocent charm of the white-trimmed windows and blooming hydrangeas. My eyes narrowed as I recognized Gina Reed, the real estate agent who had been selling Kenneth's home.

"Maude, look," I said, pointing at her. "It's Gina. What do you think she's up to?"

"Let's find out," Maude replied as her foot eased off the gas pedal. We parked a little further down the street and climbed out of the car, our curiosity piqued.

"Hello there, ladies!" Gina called out, not missing a beat as we approached. She adjusted her oversized sunglasses with one hand while flipping through a stack of papers with the other. "Are you still looking to purchase a home?"

"Hello, Gina," I greeted her cautiously. "We're just passing by. How are things?"

"Everything's fabulous," she said breezily, appearing completely unfazed by recent events. "I've got so many magnificent properties to show you two. Are you sure you're not in the market? You'd look great in a place like this."

"Thank you, but we're just here for the fresh air and scenery," Maude chimed in, glancing around with a raised eyebrow. "The neighborhood has such a lovely atmosphere, don't you think?"

"Absolutely," Gina agreed, her smile never faltering. "And it's only going to get better with the new development coming in."

"Is that so?" Maude asked, exchanging a quick glance with me.

"Of course!" Gina exclaimed, gesturing to the surrounding homes. "Just imagine all the new businesses and people that will come to the area. It's a very exciting time."

"Actually, Gina," I said, flashing a polite smile. "We're not currently in the market for a new home. We were just wondering about the fate of the homeowners affected by the development."

"Ah, I see," replied Gina, her eyes fixed on us as she adjusted her sunglasses again. "Well, it's definitely a time of change for some. But you know what they say — change can be a good thing!" She punctuated her statement with an enthusiastic nod, her perky demeanor at odds with the gravity of our investigation.

"Of course," Maude agreed dryly, her steely eyes never leaving Gina's face. "But we're really just curious about the local impacts right now."

"Understandable," Gina conceded, though I sensed a hint of disappointment in her voice. "But if you happen to reconsider, I've got some amazing properties that would be perfect for you two." She clapped her hands together, as though the mere thought of selling us a house filled her with glee.

"Like this modern loft downtown," she continued, pointing to a glossy photo on one of her papers. "It's got floor-to-ceiling windows, polished concrete floors, and even a rooftop garden! Or how about this cozy cottage by the lake? Just imagine curling up by the fireplace after a long day of... well, whatever it is you two get up to!" Gina winked conspiratorially, clearly unaware of our sleuthing activities.

As she rattled off details about the various properties, I couldn't help but notice the way her enthusiasm seemed to border on desperation. It was as though she could sense that we were onto something, and was doing her best to distract us from our true purpose.

"Thank you for the information, Gina," Maude finally interrupted, her voice firm but polite. "We'll certainly keep those properties in mind if we decide to look for a new home."

"Please do," Gina replied, her smile not quite reaching her eyes. "And call me if you have questions about the development or the neighborhood. I'm always here to help!"

"Much appreciated," I chimed in, returning her smile as best I could. As we took our leave, my thoughts raced with the implications of our conversation and the clues it contained.

"Maude, did you notice...?" I began, once we were safely back in the car.

"Her eagerness to sell us a house? Absolutely," she replied, her knitted brows showing her concern. "Something's definitely amiss here.

As we drove away, I glanced back at Gina, her gaze following us.

"Are you thinking what I'm thinking?" I asked.

Maude gripped the steering wheel tightly, generating white knuckles. "Already there," she replied.

"Another day, another dead body," I quipped to Maude as we left Gina.

"Come on, Mabel. We have work to do," Maude said, her eyes focused on the horizon as if she could already see the Mystery Book Nook before us.

"Port la Pena does sound rather lovely, doesn't it?" I mused, trying to lighten the mood. "Imagine sitting on the beach with a cocktail in hand, feeling the warm sand between your toes."

"Perhaps," Maude replied, not taking her eyes off the path ahead. "But right now, we've got a murder to solve." Her determination was infectious, but I couldn't help but let my thoughts drift for a moment.

"Of course, you're right," I agreed, steering the conversation back to the task at hand. "Though it would be nice for you to have a place closer to Nathan. And who knows, maybe there'll be grandkids in the future if we can clear his name."

Maude grinned widely. I knew those grandkids would have her completely wrapped around their tiny little fingers.

"First things first. Let's focus on Kenneth's murder." Maude's voice was both stern and kind.

We had barely entered The Mystery Book Nook when Erin greeted us with her usual enthusiasm. "Maude, Mabel! So glad you've come back."

Maude and I stopped just inside the door. "What is that?" I asked, pointing to a pig who had a cat sitting on its back.

Erin chuckled, "That's Clem and Leroy. They're kind of the mascots here." She leaned in and whispered, "I refer to them as my barnyard kids."

Would there be no end to surprises with this place?

Erin glanced back and forth between us. "Is everything OK?"

Could we trust her with our investigation? Nathan's future was at stake. And I knew Maude would leave no stone unturned to clear his name.

Maude had a particular way of walking when she was deep in thought — long strides mixed with an almost imperceptible shuffle. She ventured further into the room, looking around to see who might be near. She leaned in and said in a voice just above a whisper, "We've got some serious investigation to do."

Erin nodded. "I've got just the place for your sleuthing session," she said, gesturing for us to follow her through the maze of bookshelves.

She opened a door labeled "Private" and ushered us into a small, secluded room filled with comfy armchairs and soft lighting — a perfect spot for our clandestine discussions.

"Wow, Erin, this is perfect!" I exclaimed, taking in the cozy atmosphere.

"Thank you," she beamed. "I thought you'd like it."

As we settled into our chairs, Erin hesitated for a moment before speaking up. "You know, if you don't mind, I'd love to join you ladies today. I've been honing my investigative skills lately, and I think I could contribute something to your case." With that, she pulled out a sleek laptop and plopped down on the floor between us, her fingers poised over the keyboard. She pulled down a pair of glasses that perched on her head. The rhinestones on the frames matched her cute cowgirl boots.

Maude slightly hesitated, then said, "Of course. We appreciate all the help we can get."

Erin's face lit up at our acceptance. She turned back to her laptop and opened up a folder in the on-line forum. "If you want to talk, I can type and collect all our notes. Maybe with more details, we might get others from around the world to chime in with their theories."

"Does that really work?" I asked. "Are people with no knowledge or experience about the case actually able to help?"

Erin looked at me, tipping her head to look over the top of her glasses. "You'd be surprised. Sometimes neutrality and distance can be a benefit."

"Right you are, Erin," I agreed, watching as she pulled up various documents on her laptop screen. It seemed our little investigation was about to get a lot more interesting.

"OK, ladies," Erin announced, ready to dive headfirst into the mystery. "What do we know so far?"

"First," I chimed in, "we discovered a voided contract between Blake Stevens and Kenneth Andrews, our dearly departed neighbor. Blake seems to be the most disgruntled of Kenneth's victims since he lost quite a bit of money in their deal."

"Ah, I see," Erin mused, her fingers tapping at her laptop as she documented our findings. "And what else?"

"Kenneth's bank statements," Maude continued, her voice firm. "They're more overdrawn than a Picasso sketch. Seems like he was in dire financial straits at the time of his demise."

"Interesting," Erin commented, jotting down the information. "Any idea why?"

"None yet," I admitted, feeling a pang of frustration. It seemed like every new clue only led to more questions. "But we're determined to find out. After all, Kenneth's murder is tied to Nathan's future."

"Exactly," Maude agreed, giving me a supportive nod. "It feels like we have a lot of disparate details. Nothing by itself might show a motive, but we need to figure out how it's all tied together."

Erin looked left and right between me and Maude. "I see that you ladies are pretty experienced detectives…"

I wasn't sure how that was obvious. By all appearances, we were two elderly ladies. And we liked to keep the expectations low.

Continuing, she asked, "Have you ever used a mind map?"

Maude furrowed her brows and shook her head.

"Stan uses them all the time. Sometimes a visual can make all the difference in progress for solving a mystery."

"I'm all for anything to move this forward," Maude said and scooted to the edge of her seat.

Erin tapped several keys on the laptop and brought up a diagram that looked like a spider. "Here's how it works." She pointed to the screen. "This is one we're working on for another mystery about a painting found to be a fraud from a museum in Germany." She described the meaning of the diagram. The victim's name was placed in the center circle. Several lines extended from the center circle, each to a connecting circle at the other end. The suspect's name was placed in the outer circle with the line showing the relationship and a possible motive the suspect had for the crime.

ESTATE IN PERIL

Maude slapped her hand over her mouth.

CHAPTER TWELVE

Her eyes widened. "This is brilliant, Erin!" She leaned over Erin's shoulder and directed her to place in the outer circles the names of everyone we could think of who might be a suspect. Maude sat back in her chair and sighed heavily.

"Let's leave him off for now. It might just muddy the picture," I said. Maude always insisted we follow the evidence and clues to lead to the killer. But if that suspect was her son? How could she be impartial about that?

Maude tapped several keys on her phone. "I just sent you the pics we have of some of the evidence."

I hoped Erin didn't ask how we had acquired it. In her position, she probably learned not to question too much.

"Absolutely," Erin replied, her fingers dancing across the keyboard like a pianist playing a particularly tricky concerto. It always amazed me how fast she could type. It was mesmerizing, like watching a master at work.

As Erin uploaded the voided contract and bank statements, I couldn't help but think of the person who had created this online haven for amateur detectives. It was such a brilliant idea, bringing together like-minded individuals from all corners of the globe to solve mysteries that had left even the most seasoned professionals scratching their heads.

"Hey, look what I found!" Erin exclaimed suddenly, pulling me out of my reverie. "There's a post here from someone in France who seems to have some new information on our case."

"Really?" Maude leaned over Erin's shoulder, curious. "What does it say?"

"According to this user," Erin began, adjusting her glasses and squinting at the screen, "our dear mayor has made some rather terrible investments recently, which have led him to the brink of bankruptcy."

"Bankruptcy?" I echoed, feeling a shiver of excitement run down my spine. This was precisely the juicy detail we needed to get closer to solving Kenneth's murder. "Now that's interesting."

"Very interesting," Maude agreed, a playful grin tugging at the corners of her mouth. "It seems our esteemed mayor had more than just political reasons to conspire with Kenneth. Desperate times call for desperate measures, after all."

"Exactly," Erin chimed in, clearly thrilled to be contributing to our investigation. "And with Kenneth gone, I bet the mayor is feeling the heat."

"Let's not jump to conclusions just yet," I cautioned, ever the voice of reason. "We still need more evidence to connect the mayor to Kenneth's murder."

"True," Maude conceded. "But this new information certainly adds another layer to our case."

"Indeed, it does," I agreed, my mind already racing with the possibilities. "Let's add him to our diagram." I wasn't convinced the picture would help guide us to the answer in this case. If nothing else, it had become more complicated.

Maude's phone buzzed. I squeezed my eyes shut, hoping it wasn't Nathan with bad news.

She held it up and said, "Eureka!" That was our code word for "gold mine." "I knew my girl Steph would come through."

Erin looked at me. "Maude used to be a cybersecurity analyst," I said, as if that were all the explanation needed.

"Stephanie found some dirt on Blake. Besides being scammed and being in over his head financially with the development, he actually has another family in another state."

Erin stood and placed her laptop on the table, stretching her arms overhead. "What?"

"Yeah. It's not clear if it's a secret from his current family or not. But judging by the way the out-of-state family lives, he provides very well for them financially." Maude stood next to Erin.

This just might be the straw that broke this whole thing wide open. "Is it time to go to the police with this?" I asked.

Maude flopped back down into the comfy chair. Providing the police what we had to date likely meant we would need to step back and let them take over from here. Would Maude be able to relinquish control? I didn't see that happening, given the stakes.

"All roads seem to lead to Blake," I breathed.

Maude tapped her cheek. "They do. But something about it seems so obvious. Like, too obvious."

Erin brought up the spider diagram again as we slowly walked through each suspect and motive. "Let's be sure we've been thorough with what we have first."

"Good idea. Taking something half-baked to the police may discredit anything we offer," Maude said.

One by one, we discussed everything we knew about each suspect. Erin took meticulous notes on our thoughts surrounding motive and how the suspect might have crossed paths with Kenneth. While a more thorough picture, it didn't clarify any further who we should point the finger at.

"I think we've exhausted all our efforts. Maybe it's time to turn this over to the professionals," I said. Maude and I had yet to yield one of our investigations. This felt like defeat.

My phone buzzed loudly on the table, interrupting our intense sleuthing session. I glanced at the screen and sighed. "It's Gina," I said, rolling my eyes. "I swear, that woman is more tenacious than a bloodhound."

"Answer it," Maude suggested, smirking. "You never know. She might have some useful information. Or a fabulous vacation home in Port la Pena."

"Hilarious," I retorted, but answered the call. "Hello, Gina. I'm going to put you on speaker." I punched the speaker icon and Gina's voice filled the room.

"Ah, Mabel, darling! I'm so glad I caught you," Gina gushed, her voice dripping with saccharine sweetness. "I simply must meet with you and Maude for lunch tomorrow. I've found the most perfect property for you two — it's got everything you could ever want in a vacation home!"

"Really, Gina, we're quite busy right now —" I tried to brush her off, but she bulldozed right over me.

"Of course, of course, I understand completely," she purred. "But this is a once-in-a-lifetime opportunity, Mabel. You don't want to miss out on your dream vacation home, do you? Just one quick meeting."

I glanced at Maude, who shrugged, a bemused smile playing across her lips. I sighed, knowing full well that Gina wouldn't take no for an answer. "Fine, Gina. We can meet you tomorrow, but make it quick."

"Marvelous!" Gina chirped. "I'll text you the address. See you tomorrow!"

As I hung up, I couldn't help but wonder if Gina's real estate prowess might somehow come in handy for our investigation.

"Alright, we'll meet her tomorrow," I told Maude. "But I swear, if she tries to sell an overpriced fixer-upper, I'm going to lose my mind."

"Relax, Mabel," Maude chuckled, her eyes twinkling with mischief. "Who knows? Maybe we'll find the clue that cracks this case wide open in the wine cellar of our new vacation home."

"Ha! In that case, I'll gladly endure Gina's sales pitch," I replied, grinning.

Erin closed her laptop as Vangie entered the room. "How's it going? You all done?" She looked expectantly at each of us.

"It's hard to tell," Maude said. "But we certainly learned a new technique for cataloging our information. Erin is an expert at this."

Vangie beamed. "Yes, she is.

Erin tucked her laptop under her arm. "We have a prime suspect. We think."

"Blake Stevens," I said. Although saying it out loud didn't bring any sense of accomplishment. My gut gurgled with some kind of clue that said this just wasn't right.

Vangie stepped back. "No way." She put her hand over her heart. "I mean, he seems sleazy, but a murderer?" Shaking her head, she continued. "There's been rumors at the business rotary meeting that he and the mayor were in cahoots with that development. But murder?" Her voice trailed off.

I nodded in agreement. "It doesn't feel right. Too easy, you know? But we don't have any other leads at the moment." I leaned back in my chair, letting out a frustrated sigh.

Maude furrowed her brow. "Maybe it's time we start thinking outside the box. We've been so focused on the suspects and their motives that we might be missing something else."

Erin nodded eagerly. "Yes, let's brainstorm. What else could have happened to Kenneth?"

Vangie leaned against the wall, deep in thought. "Well, what about the property itself? Maybe there's something there that could give us a clue."

I perked up at the suggestion. "That's not a bad idea. We know Kenneth was working on the development. Maybe he uncovered something he shouldn't have."

Maude stood up, pacing around the room. "But what could it be? A hidden treasure? Some kind of illegal activity?"

Erin's eyes widened. "What if it's not about the property itself, but something that happened on it? Like, maybe there's a buried body or something."

Vangie let out a nervous laugh. "OK, let's not jump to conclusions here. But it's worth exploring. Maybe we should go out to the property and see if we can find anything."

I nodded, feeling a renewed sense of purpose.

Maude's phone buzzed. I was hopeful it was more from Steph that might just seal the deal on Blake. Or if not Blake, then someone else. We had to be close. I could feel it in my old bones.

"Argh!" Maude said. "It's Gina again." She answered, abruptly. "Yes?" Maude frowned. She held out her phone without turning on the speaker.

"I've found another house, just perfect for you. You must see it when we meet tomorrow," Gina said.

"I don't know, Gina. We're pretty busy. We might not make it," Maude said.

Gina exuded something between a gasp and a squeal as her voice jumped several octaves. "You have to!" she ordered. With a calmer voice, she followed up. "I mean. I think you would really love it. And I wouldn't want you to miss out on an opportunity to have a place closer to Nathan."

Maude rolled her eyes.

I could tell Maude was done with Gina's pushy sales tactics. "Fine, we'll try to make it. But don't expect anything," she said, before hanging up.

"I'm thinking Gina might be more trouble than she's worth," I said, feeling a twinge of annoyance.

Vangie shrugged. "Maybe, but she could still be useful. We can always use more information, even if it's coming from someone like her."

I couldn't help but feel a sense of unease. Gina's sudden interest in finding us a vacation home seemed suspicious, and I couldn't shake the feeling that there was something more to her incessant calls.

"We need to keep an eye on Gina," I said, voicing my concerns. "She might be involved in this in some way."

Erin opened her laptop and added a leg to the diagram and added Gina's name to the circle.

"I doubt it," Vangie said. "That's just how she is. Pushy."

"She used to be one of the top sellers in real estate in this area before the development," Erin added.

"She's probably just trying to get back to that top spot," Vangie said.

Maude and I grabbed our bags. We certainly needed some decompression time at the cottage. A stiff drink on the deck overlooking the ocean was just what the doctor ordered.

CHAPTER THIRTEEN

"Morning," Maude muttered, her voice gravelly from sleep. "Didn't get much rest last night. My mind's been racing about this case. We're no closer to clearing Nathan's name."

I swung my legs over the side of the bed, the memory of her son's worried face propelling me into action. "Let's go over what we know so far."

We shuffled into the small kitchen, our slippers scuffing against the linoleum as we prepared our morning cups of tea. The scent of Earl Grey filled the air, providing a momentary comfort amid the chaos.

Mindlessly stirring some honey into my tea, I said, "What do we have, and what do we still need to discover?"

"Good question." Maude tapped her finger on the counter, deep in thought. "We know Kenneth had enemies, and we've found several people who lost money to him. However, we don't have any concrete proof tying anyone to the murder."

"Exactly." I sighed, sipping my tea. "We're missing a crucial piece of the puzzle. We need to find a connection between the scam, the murder, and someone with a motive. Or perhaps several someones," I suggested, recalling the many shady characters we'd encountered during our investigation. "We can't rule out a conspiracy."

Maude's eyes twinkled with excitement. "Now there's an intriguing thought! We could be dealing with a whole web of deceit here." Maude gripped her cup with both hands and wandered to the sliding glass door, gazing out at the cloud covered ocean. She bundled up her robe and opened the door. I followed her outside as we sat in the cooler morning air, a slight mist washing over our faces.

"Maude," I said, turning to face her, "I've been thinking... we can't just sit on all this information. We've uncovered so much during our investigation. Maybe it's time to involve the police."

"Perhaps you're right," she finally conceded, setting her cup aside, leaning back in the lounge chair, and closing her eyes. "We've tried our best to unravel this tangled web, but we could use some help from the professionals."

"Exactly," I replied, relieved that she agreed. "And who knows? Maybe they've discovered something we haven't. It's worth a shot."

"Very well," Maude said, standing up and tugging the belt on her robe. "Let's pay a visit to the police station. But first, we should check in on Nathan. He must be feeling overwhelmed by all of this."

"Agreed," I said, grabbing my cup of tea. "He needs to know we're doing everything we can to clear his name."

Maude sat up in her chair and shivered. I couldn't imagine the stress she was experiencing because of a family member smack dab in the middle of a murder investigation. I had only met Nathan on this trip. But from what I saw, there was no way he was involved in this. He seemed genuinely upset about Kenneth's murder, despite their tumultuous relationship.

We finished our tea in silence and got ready for our trip to Nathan's to see how he was holding up. This had turned into one of our most challenging cases yet.

As we turned a corner, my heart skipped a beat. A police car was parked in front of Blake's house. I glanced at Maude, who was wearing an expression that mirrored my surprise.

"Maude, do you think they're finally arresting Blake for Kenneth's murder?" I asked, trying to contain my excitement.

"Could be," she replied with a grin. "The investigation must have been moving quicker than we thought."

"Or maybe our snooping around has sped things up," I offered, feeling a surge of pride.

"Perhaps," Maude mused. "Either way, this is excellent news. Once Blake is arrested, Nathan's name might finally be cleared."

We continued on our way to Nathan's place, our spirits lifted at the sight of the police car. As we approached his house, I felt a strange mix of relief and anticipation. What would happen next? And how could we find out what was actually going on?

"Deep breaths, Mabel," Maude reminded me gently as we knocked on Nathan's door. "We're almost there."

Nathan opened the door, looking tired but relieved to see us. "Mom, Mabel, I'm glad to see you."

Maude turned and pointed down the street to the police car. Nathan poked his head out the door and looked at Maude.

We all stepped inside, and Maude said, "I think Blake is being arrested. Why else would they be there?"

"Mom, what have you been doing?" Nathan led us to the living room. "I asked you to stay out of it and let the police do their job."

"Now, dear," Maude started. How much would she reveal about our escapades? I expected we knew a lot more than Nathan realized about this case.

"Maude, Mabel," Mollie said, entering and sitting next to Nathan. "Nice to see you. How is your sightseeing going?"

"We've seen a lot. Including all the people upset at this new development happening near the beach," I replied.

Mollie nodded. "Yes, it's been quite contentious."

"How are you doing, Nathan?" Maude asked.

He sat back in his seat and ran his hand through his hair. "I'm all right. If Blake is actually being arrested, I might sleep better." He heaved an enormous sigh.

Maude glanced at me and back at Nathan. "We happened to find out some things that seem to provide some pretty solid evidence against Blake. Looks like the police might have discovered it too if they are at his house arresting him."

Nathan glanced at Mollie, and she slightly nodded. Nathan hesitated before speaking. "There's something I need to tell you both. I didn't want to say anything earlier, but... Kenneth scammed me out of a lot of money, too."

"Scammed you?!" Maude exclaimed, her face turning a shade of red I'd only seen when her favorite mystery novels were out of stock at the local bookstore. "Why on earth didn't you tell me, Nathan?"

"Mom, I didn't want to worry you," he replied, his voice cracking. "You've been through enough without having to deal with my problems."

"Sweetheart," Maude said, her anger dissolving into concern, "we're a team. You can't keep things like this from us, especially when it's related to a murder investigation we're trying to solve!"

"She's right," I chimed in, placing a supportive hand on Nathan's arm. "We're here for you, no matter what."

"Thank you," Nathan whispered, his eyes brimming with tears. "I don't know what I'd do without you both."

Mollie stood. "Why don't I get us some coffee?"

I retrieved a tissue from my purse and handed it to Nathan. The stress from the ordeal spilled down onto his cheeks. He shuddered a breath.

Maude's phone started buzzing in her pocket, breaking the silence of the cozy living room. She pulled it out and rolled her eyes. That could only mean one thing.

"Hi, Gina," Maude said.

The voice on the other end was so loud we could hear her without the speaker on. Gina was frantic, barely stopping to take a breath. "You and Mabel need to come over right away. There's a new property for sale, and it's perfect for you two!"

"Whoa, slow down there, Gina." Maude held the phone slightly away from her ear, no doubt trying to protect her eardrums from the agent's enthusiasm. "Why the urgency?"

"Trust me, this house won't last long on the market. It's an incredible opportunity, and I know how much you two love Port la Pena. You've got to see it today!" Gina's voice reached an almost feverish pitch.

"Alright, alright," Maude conceded, shaking her head as she continued to talk to Gina. "Give us the address, and we'll be there as soon as we can."

Gina rattled off the location, and Maude scribbled it down on a notepad that Nathan handed her before hanging up the phone. "Well, Mabel, it looks like our little adventure isn't over yet. Gina seems to think she's found the perfect place for us."

"Can you believe the nerve of that woman?" I grumbled.

"You're buying a house here?" Nathan asked.

Maude grinned. "Maybe. I thought having a vacation home here might be fun and give us more of a chance to visit."

Nathan stood and hugged his mom tight. No matter how old you got, it could be nice to have your mom around.

Maude's phone buzzed again. "Argh!" she growled, likely suspecting it was Gina. I supposed that was' how she got to be a top seller, persistence. Although it came across as badgering.

She glanced down and tapped the screen, her eyes scanning the notification. "Interesting," Maude muttered under her breath, clearly distracted by whatever she was reading.

"Something useful for our investigation?" I asked, craning my neck to sneak a peek at the message.

"No, it's a contract that Erin uploaded to our folder at The Mystery Book Nook forum. Apparently, Gina's trying to take twice the normal commission on this property — some financial troubles, it seems." Maude shook her head, her lips pressed into a thin line. "I'll have to keep an eye on her during our meeting."

"Ah, good old-fashioned greed," I mused. "Well, it wouldn't be the first time we've dealt with someone's less-than-honorable intentions."

Mollie arrived with our coffee, and we sat silently sipping it, trying to relieve some of the tension that had built over the last few days of this investigation. Could we really relax now with Blake's arrest? Maude and I would likely extend our visit a few more days so we could enjoy some time with Nathan and Mollie without the threat of Nathan being arrested hanging over our heads.

The phone call with Gina played on a loop in my head. I couldn't shake the feeling that there was something off about her insistence for us to view the property immediately. Was it simply because of her financial troubles, or was there more to the story?

A loud knock on the door prompted Nathan to slosh his coffee out of his cup. Mollie ran to get a towel as Nathan stood.

My heart leapt into my throat, and I exchanged panicked glances with Maude. Who could it be?

"Stay here," she instructed, her voice low and tense. "I'll handle this."

As she approached the door, I couldn't help but feel a sense of dread wash over me.

I didn't know what to expect when Maude cautiously opened the door, but it sure wasn't a handful of police officers standing on the doorstep. The uniforms were starched and crisp, like they'd just come from the dry cleaners.

"Ma'am," one officer said, addressing Maude with a stern expression, "we're here to see Nathan."

Mollie rushed back into the room. "What's going on?" Her voice quavered.

Placing my cup on a side table, I stood and grabbed Nathan's arm. "It'll be OK," I whispered with more confidence than I felt.

Maude stepped to the side and let them in. The lead officer moved closer to Nathan.

"Nathan Henley, you're under arrest for the murder of Kenneth Andrews." The officer read him his Miranda rights.

My stomach churned. What in the world did they have that pointed toward Nathan? Maude and I had come up with enough evidence pointing elsewhere that this just had to be a case of mistaken identity.

"Absurd!" Maude huffed indignantly, adjusting her glasses like she was trying to see some sense in this situation. "Nathan would never harm a fly, let alone commit murder."

"Mom, it's OK." Nathan appeared behind Maude, his calm demeanor contrasting with the whirlwind of emotions swirling around us. "I'll go with them. We'll sort everything out."

"Are you sure?" Maude asked, her brow furrowed with worry.

"Of course," Nathan reassured her, placing a steady hand on her shoulder. "It's all just a big misunderstanding."

"Very well, then." Maude reluctantly stepped aside, allowing the police to handcuff her son.

Mollie sniffled. "Maude, do something."

CHAPTER FOURTEEN

The reason for Nathan's arrest remained a mystery. The police didn't share the evidence they had. But there was no denying the sinking feeling that we had missed a critical clue.

I retrieved a glass of water from the kitchen. "Here, Mollie," I said softly, handing her a glass. Maude gently took hold of Mollie's free hand and led her to sit down.

"Thanks, Mabel. Thank you, Maude," Mollie whispered, taking a sip of water before gulping down a deep breath. "I just can't believe this is happening."

Maude looked up at me. I knew she was itching to get on with the investigation. I slightly nodded. "Mollie, Maude and I have some business to take care of. Will you be OK for a bit?"

Mollie looked wide-eyed at us like a deer in the headlights. I hated to leave her, but we had to pursue our instincts, hoping to get Nathan freed.

Maude patted Mollie's hand. "We'll stop in and see Nathan. We'll keep you posted."

My heart hurt for that girl. I couldn't imagine your loved one being taken away in handcuffs for any reason, but murder? That was too much.

Her phone buzzing in her pocket, Maude just shook her head and ignored it. Likely it was the pushy Gina wanting to know where we were.

Silently, we stood and hugged as Maude and I left Mollie. As we exited the house, we both exhaled, scurrying to our car. Maude jammed it into gear and sped away.

"Easy there, girl. We have to remain alive in order to solve this thing," I said.

As we drove through the quaint streets of the small town, I couldn't help but feel like we were inching closer to unraveling the mystery surrounding Kenneth's murder. But first, we had to get through this appointment with Gina without letting on that we suspected her of any wrongdoing.

"Remember," Maude cautioned, "keep the conversation focused on the house. We don't want her to know we're digging into her background."

"Got it."

Maude gripped the steering wheel a little tighter, her knuckles turning as white as the cotton candy clouds drifted lazily across the sky.

"Here," Maude handed her phone to me. "Why don't you look at that contract just to see if there's something I missed?"

"Look at this," I said. "Clause 8.3 states that if the buyer cancels the transaction after signing the purchase agreement, the seller is still obligated to pay Gina's full commission."

"Goodness gracious!" Maude exclaimed. "That doesn't seem fair at all."

"Fair or not, it's definitely unusual," I said. "And here's another one: Clause 12.5 says that Gina is entitled to a bonus commission if the property sells for more than its asking price."

"Isn't that like a double-dipping of sorts?" Maude asked, her eyebrows knitting together in confusion.

"Indeed, it is," I agreed. "It seems like Gina has found a way to squeeze every last penny out of her clients." Maude had stepped up the pace as we zoomed through the streets, nearing our destination.

As we continued down the road, my mind churned with thoughts about Gina's financial situation. What could have led her to cheat people out of extra commissions? Maude seemed to think along the same lines.

"Remember when we first met Gina?" she asked. "She wore that dress that looked like it was for the red carpet and those flashy diamond earrings."

"Ah, yes," I recalled, the image of Gina's ostentatious attire seared into my mind. "Like she was headed to the academy awards ceremony."

"Exactly," Maude nodded. "And although it's not unusual for successful real estate agents to drive up-scale cars, the one she had was at the top of the line. It's as if she's living beyond her means."

"Could it be that she's desperate for money?" I wondered aloud. "Maybe she's drowning in debt, or perhaps there's some sort of expensive vice she's trying to maintain."

"Both are possibilities," Maude conceded. "But we need more concrete evidence before we can make any definitive conclusions."

As we pulled up to the house that Gina wanted to show us, a feeling of unease settled into the pit of my stomach.

The house was nestled in a picturesque cul-de-sac, surrounded by well-manicured lawns and flowerbeds bursting with vibrant colors. As we pulled into the driveway, I couldn't help but admire the charming exterior: a fresh coat of butter-yellow paint adorned the siding, and a cheerful red door seemed to beckon us inside.

"Maude," I said as she turned off the car, "we shouldn't forget that Gina was the one who discovered Kenneth's body."

"Ah, yes," Maude replied.

"Indeed," I agreed with a shudder. "Poor Kenneth."

"It seems rather... convenient, doesn't it?"

"It does," I admitted. "And speaking of which, I remember her emotional state after discovering the body being peculiar. She seemed distraught, as anyone would be, but there was something else - an undercurrent of agitation, almost as if she were hiding something."

"Interesting..." Maude mused. "Could you be more specific about her behavior? What exactly did she say or do that caught your attention?"

"Her eyes kept darting around nervously," I replied, recalling the scene vividly. "And she repeatedly insisted that she had nothing to do with Kenneth's death, even though no one had accused her of any wrongdoing. It struck me as defensive and suspicious."

"Definitely worth noting," Maude said, nodding. "I didn't notice that at the time."

As we approached the front door, Gina greeted us with a wide smile, her eyes darting around as if searching for potential eavesdroppers. "Hello! Welcome to this enchanting piece of history. Shall we begin the tour?"

"Of course," Maude replied, her voice steady and professional. "Lead the way."

"Alright," Gina said, opening the door and ushering us inside. "Now, I must warn you that this house has quite a few... quirks. But I'm sure you'll find it absolutely delightful!"

"Quirks, you say?" I mused, already intrigued by the prospect of uncovering hidden secrets in the home. "Well, we are no strangers to peculiarities, are we, Maude?"

"Indeed not," Maude replied, her eyes alight with mischief. "In fact, we relish the opportunity to explore the unusual and unexpected."

"Then you're in for a treat," Gina said, her voice taking on an air of mystery as she led us through the house.

"Come on in," Gina beckoned, leading us through the enormous double doors into a breathtaking foyer. The high ceilings were adorned with intricate moldings and an elaborate chandelier that sparkled like a thousand diamonds.

"Ooh, fancy," I murmured, taking in the opulent surroundings.

"Quite," Maude agreed, her eyes darting around, undoubtedly looking for anything out of the ordinary.

"Let me give you a quick tour," Gina said, clasping her hands together in excitement. She pointed out room after room, each more luxurious than the last. "And this is the gourmet kitchen, complete with top-of-the-line appliances and enough counter space to host your own cooking show!"

"Marvelous," I sighed, imagining myself whipping up culinary masterpieces while wearing a frilly apron. Maude snorted, clearly not sharing my fantasy.

"Alright, let's get down to business," Gina chirped, pulling out a contract from her sleek leather briefcase. "I just need your signatures right here, agreeing to double the commission. It'll come out to exactly $60,000."

"Sixty thousand dollars?" Maude spluttered, her eyebrows shooting up to her hairline. "That's preposterous!"

"Is that... typical?" I asked hesitantly, trying to wrap my head around the exorbitant amount.

"Absolutely!" Gina insisted, flashing us a dazzling smile. "For high-end homes like this, it's completely normal. Trust me, it's worth every penny." She flipped her hair back like she was in a modelling shoot.

I glanced over at Maude, who was currently scrutinizing the contract with the intensity of a hawk. Her face remained impassive, but I could practically hear the gears of her analytical mind whirring away.

"Excuse me for a moment, ladies," Gina said with a smile that seemed more plastic than genuine. She pulled her phone from her pocket and hurried out of the room, leaving Maude and me standing in the lavish kitchen.

We stood in silence for a moment, straining our ears to catch any snippets of conversation from Gina's phone call. It wasn't long before we heard her voice, muffled but still discernable, drift back into the room.

"Listen, I'll get the money as soon as I can, alright? I've got two live wires on the line, and they're practically eating out of my hand." There was a pause, during which Maude and I exchanged a knowing look. "No, no, don't worry. They won't suspect a thing."

"Live wires?" I whispered, my heart pounding in my chest. "That's us, isn't it?"

"Seems like it," Maude confirmed, her expression darkening. "And I don't like what this implies about Gina's intentions."

"Neither do I," I admitted, my fingers nervously tapping against the granite countertop. "We need to tread carefully here, Maude. If Gina's involved in some kind of shady business, we could be in real danger."

"Agreed," she said, her eyes narrowing even further as she considered our next move. "But we're not backing down, Mabel. Whatever Gina's hiding, we're going to uncover it — Nathan's freedom depends on it."

Gina breezed back into the room, her smile as bright as ever. "Sorry about that, ladies," she chirped. "Now, where were we?"

"Ah yes," I said, forcing a grin onto my face. "Can we see the backyard?" I asked, desperate for an escape from the confined space and the mounting pressure.

"Absolutely!" Gina replied cheerfully, guiding me through the French doors and onto a sprawling patio.

"Isn't this just perfect for hosting parties?" Gina enthused, clasping her hands together. "Imagine all the fun you could have out here!"

Or all the bodies you could hide, I thought grimly, taking in the tall hedges and secluded corners of the garden. Was Gina really capable of murder?

"Sorry, I'm not much of a party person," I confessed, forcing another polite smile. "But it is quite lovely."

"Isn't it?" Gina sighed dreamily. "Well, let's head back inside. There's so much more to show you!"

As we turned to leave the backyard, my eyes caught Maude's tense figure through the window, her fingers still flying across her phone screen as if our lives depended on it. The knot in my stomach tightened — clearly, she was as worried about our situation as I was.

"Is your friend OK?" Gina asked, a hint of concern creeping into her voice. "She seems rather... preoccupied."

"Oh, she's fine," I assured her, trying to sound light-hearted. "She's just making dinner plans for us later."

"Ah, I see," Gina said, her smile returning as she stomped back into the house. "Well, let's get down to brass tacks, shall we?"

"Indeed," I murmured, glancing sidelong at Maude. Her eyes were sharp as ever, scanning the room like a hawk.

"Here's the contract," Gina said, thrusting it towards us. "I just need your signatures right here, and we'll be done."

"Already?" asked Maude, raising an eyebrow. "Don't we want to read it first?" I mean, who knows what kind of chicanery might lurk in there?"

"Chicanery?" Gina laughed, a touch too loudly. "My dear ladies, I assure you, this is a standard contract. Nothing suspicious or underhanded, I promise."

"Be that as it may," I interjected, "we'd still like a moment to peruse the document."

"Very well," she sighed, handing over the contract with a flourish. "But do hurry, won't you? Time is of the essence, after all."

"Of course," Maude replied sweetly, her eyes already darting over the fine print.

I watched as Gina shifted from foot to foot, her agitation growing by the second.

"Actually," Maude said suddenly, her eyes sparkling with mischief, "this house is growing on me. Mabel, what do you think? Shall we make an offer?"

I had no idea where Maude was going with this, but I played along. "I agree."

Maude paced in a circle around the room.

"Excellent!" Gina clapped her hands together, clearly relieved by our sudden change of heart. "Let's get that contract signed, shall we?"

"Actually," Maude interjected again, much to Gina's dismay, "I'd like to take another look at the contract, if you don't mind."

Gina's brow furrowed as she hesitated for a moment, her smile shaky. "OK, just hurry."

"Thank you," Maude said graciously, settling into an armchair, contract in hand.

As Maude began poring over the document once more, I couldn't help but notice Gina's increasing agitation. She paced back and forth, wringing her hands and casting anxious glances our way.

"Actually," I chimed in, feigning nonchalance, "we might be interested in seeing that other house later. But first, we should finish up here."

"Fine," Gina snapped, her veneer of professionalism cracking just enough to betray her mounting frustration. "But let's wrap this up quickly, shall we?" This woman couldn't have been more obviously desperate to get her hot little hands on our money.

"Of course," Maude agreed, but she continued to take her time, meticulously scanning the fine print on the contract. I could tell that Gina was growing more and more agitated with each passing moment, which only fueled our desire to uncover what she was hiding.

"Alright, that's it!" Gina exclaimed suddenly, snatching the contract from Maude's hands. Her face was flushed with anger, her eyes darting back and forth between Maude and me. "I have other appointments today, you know. I can't spend all day waiting for you two old biddies to make up your minds."

"Apologies," Maude replied coolly, unfazed by Gina's outburst. "We didn't mean to keep you from your other clients. Please, feel free to leave if you must."

"Fine," Gina huffed, tucking the contract under her arm and marching towards the front door. "But I expect a decision from you two soon. I can't hold this house forever, you know."

That's when we heard footsteps approaching, followed by a knock on the door. Gina's face went white as a sheet.

CHAPTER FIFTEEN

"Mercy me," I muttered, glancing out the front window and spotting a police car parked outside Gina's cozy little bungalow. "Gina, your guests have arrived."

"Guests? What guests?" Gina asked, her voice cracking. She peeked out from behind the kitchen curtain and saw the flashing blue and red lights reflecting off the well-manicured lawn. Her eyes widened in panic.

In that instant, she decided her only option was to make a run for it. She dashed towards the back door, kicking off her heels.

"Wait, Gina!" I called after her, but she was already turning the doorknob and bolting into the backyard like a frightened hare.

As she sprinted through the garden, trampling the prized rose bushes, I couldn't help but dwell on what had brought us here. Poor Kenneth, with terrible taste in business partners, had met his untimely end, and Gina, who had simply been trying to reclaim the money he'd swindled from her, now found herself the prime suspect in his murder.

Maude opened the front door and alerted the officers that Gina had attempted an escape through the backyard.

"Thanks for the heads-up, ma'am," an officer responded, speaking into his radio.

"Be careful! She seemed quite desperate," I warned them, adding just enough drama to ensure they took the situation seriously.

"Appreciate the tip." He tipped his cap before both officers sprinted around the side of the house.

Maude and I stepped onto the front porch. "Mabes, I hope we did the right thing. I feel in my gut she was responsible for Kenneth's death."

I grabbed Maude's hand. "We did. Why would she run if she wasn't guilty of something? All the pieces fit. We just didn't see it in the beginning."

We stepped from the porch to the front lawn. Nothing to do now except wait.

Sure enough, I heard a commotion coming from the back of the house. It sounded like a scuffle, followed by a woman's voice shouting out in protest.

"I didn't do it, I swear!" The voice was unmistakably Gina's, and it was laced with desperation.

"Keep your hands where we can see them!" one of the officers barked.

"Please, you've got to believe me!" Gina pleaded, her voice cracking. "Kenneth scammed me out of so much money! I just... I needed it to pay off my gambling debts!"

"Save it for the judge," the officer replied coldly, cuffing Gina's hands behind her back and tucking her into the backseat of his cruiser.

"She must have felt so desperate. But murder?" Maude said.

I reached for the door behind us and locked it, gazing back at the beauty. It really would be a lovely place to own. Having a place here to stay when we came to see Nathan would be a real treat. And we could probably use it as a vacation rental when we weren't here. "You know, Maude," I started.

"Yes. I was thinking the same thing. This would make a great purchase," she said.

I couldn't shake the image of Gina's tear-streaked face pressed against the police car window and wonder how she would fare in jail. Likely not well. Maude and I headed to the car and on our way to see Nathan. I could only imagine the joyous reunion that would take place between mother and son.

We parked our car and entered the bustling lobby, where officers scurried about, carrying stacks of paperwork and barking orders into their radios.

"Look, there's Gina," I whispered to Maude, nodding my head toward the booking area.

"Miss Reed, I'm sorry, but we don't offer special privileges," the officer responded with a sigh, clearly exhausted by her incessant demands. He led her away, her designer heels covered in grass clacking indignantly against the linoleum floor.

"Goodness, that woman has some nerve," Maude remarked, shaking her head in disbelief. "She's lucky she's even here to ask for special privileges after what happened."

"Indeed," I agreed, my eyes following Gina as she disappeared down the hallway.

With Gina's dramatic departure still fresh in our minds, Maude and I barely had a moment to catch our breath before the heavy metal door at the back of the station swung open. In strode Nathan, looking no worse for wear but clearly relieved to be released.

"Mom. Mabel. Thank goodness you're here," Nathan said, embracing his mother.

"Your release couldn't come soon enough," Maude replied, her eyes brimming with tears. "You wouldn't believe the shenanigans we've witnessed since you were arrested."

Nathan plopped onto a bench lining the wall. Maude regaled him of our efforts to gain evidence against Gina once she sprinted to the top of our suspect list. Nathan just shook his head.

"Wow, sounds like quite the spectacle," Nathan remarked once Maude finished her recap. "But Mom, don't you think it's time to hang up your detective hat? You've done more than enough to help solve this case."

"Retire?" Maude scoffed, her brow furrowed in indignation. "Why, I'm just getting started! Besides, Mabel and I make a formidable team, don't you agree, dear?"

"Absolutely," I concurred, pride swelling within me. We may have been an unconventional duo, but we were undeniably effective.

"Look, I know you enjoy this, but sometimes I worry about you two getting mixed up in all this dangerous business," Nathan confessed, concern etched on his face.

"Dear boy, life is full of risks," Maude replied, patting her son's arm reassuringly. "But Mabel and I are nothing if not resourceful. We'll be just fine."

Nathan sighed as he rubbed the back of his neck, knowing it was futile to argue with his mother's ironclad determination. "Alright, well speaking of staying busy, have you two found a house you like yet? Are you planning on moving?"

Maude and I exchanged a glance, a flicker of excitement crossing our features.

"Would it sweeten the pot if I told you that you might get some grandkids soon?" Nathan ventured, a nervous smile playing at the corners of his mouth. My heart leaped into my throat, and I shot him an incredulous look.

"Are you saying that Mollie is…" Maude began, her voice trembling with excitement.

"Yep," Nathan confirmed, his grin widening. "She's pregnant!" He looked around the room, chuckling. "Though this isn't where I wanted you to learn the news."

Maude clapped her hands together and let out a joyous laugh. "This is marvelous news! Simply marvelous! Oh, I can hardly wait to spoil my little grandbaby rotten!"

"Congratulations, Nathan," I said warmly, leaning in to give him a tight hug. "You and Mollie are going to be wonderful parents!"

"Thanks, Mabel," he replied, returning the embrace. "I just hope we can survive the sleepless nights and diaper changes."

"Ah, but that's all part of the adventure, isn't it?" Maude chimed in, her eyes sparkling with anticipation. "Besides, you might just have us old birds around to lend a hand now and then."

"That would be wonderful," Nathan said, his eyes tearing up.

"Indeed," I agreed. "And who knows? Perhaps they will take an interest in mystery-solving and join us on our escapades one day."

"Ha!" Nathan laughed, shaking his head in mock exasperation. "I wouldn't put it past you two to recruit them straight out of the cradle."

"Perish the thought!" Maude feigned shock, placing a hand over her heart. "We would never dream of subjecting innocent babes to such nefarious deeds."

"Of course not," I added, giving Nathan a playful wink. "But perhaps in time, they might fancy themselves a bit of amateur sleuthing under the watchful eyes of their doting grandmother."

"Alright, alright," Nathan conceded, rolling his eyes good-naturedly. "Just be sure to let them have some fun too, OK?"

"Absolutely, dear," Maude replied, her smile softening. "After all, what's life without a little laughter and joy?"

About the Author

Sue Hollowell is a wife and empty nester with a lot of mom left over. Not far from her everyday thoughts are dreams of visiting tropical locations. She likes cake and the more frosting the better!

Manufactured by Amazon.ca
Bolton, ON